Olé! Posole!
& Other Tummy Tales

"I knew then that a new family leyenda had been born. Both the song and the soup would forever be etched in my memory. I knew that although times could be hard, there was 'Olé!' It was a word of magic and hope and familia, a word to help us smile. My extended family spanned many generations and came from many different places. But 'Olé!' meant the same thing for all of us. There is always a new day, a birthday, a new beginning, a new reason to rejoice."

SCFD
Scientific & Cultural
Facilities District

Rocky Mountain
Storytellers' Conference

This project is supported in part by a grant from the Adams County Cultural
Council Scientific and Cultural Facilities District. The SCFD is a program
dedicated to promoting art and culture in Colorado. For more information about
their programs and grants, call 303-860-0588

Editor: Ed Winograd
Ed.Winograd@gmail.com

Artist: Arlette Lucero
ArletteLuc@msn.com

Graphic Design: Michael Polk
abercfitchco@aol.com

Printing: Quality Press, Denver, CO
Printed in U.S.A.

Just Enjoyable Memorable Story Books
JEMS Books - Arvada, CO
jemsbooks@hotmail.com
ISBN 0-9724472-3-7

Olé! Posole!
& Other Tummy Tales

Compiled by
Renee Fajardo
&
Carl Ruby

Edited by
Ed Winograd

Illustrated by
Arlette Lucero

Design by
Michael Polk

JEMS Books · Arvada, Colorado

To my "daddy" and my mamma. Two young people who came from very different places and traveled very different paths. I remember only the love and goodness you both gave to me and others. Your kindness and compassion for all people of all cultures has made me who I am today. I thank you both for the gift of insight and understanding. May good food, great stories, and lots of love bless us all.

- Renee Fajardo

Dedicated to my brother, Willy, and my sisters, Carol and Sharon, for without them my childhood and adult life would be void of happy memories, caring, sharing, and love. Siblings are friends that you do not choose. Danke schön for all the times we have enjoyed and those pleasant times yet to come.

- Carl E. Ruby

I would like to dedicate this book to my parents. To my father Alex, to whom I owe my artistic talent, and whose paintings I always enjoy. To my mother Priscilla, who always believed in me and loves me no matter what.

- Arlette Lucero

Table of Contents

Summer Vacation on a One-Hundred Acre Farm

by Carl Ruby

"No more school! No more books! No more teacher's dirty looks!"
"No more school! No more books! No more teacher's ...."

As school bus #8 bounced down the dirt roads in the central New York countryside on the last day of school, that song was on everyone's lips, in our ears, and in our hearts.

I could hardly wait to jump off that rattling, noisy, old school bus. It was summer vacation! I could see that my brother Willy and my sisters Carol and Sharon were just as eager as I was.

When Old 8 stopped at our farm, we blasted out the door. A quick wave and a "Have a good summer" to Mr. Duell, the driver, and we were gone. We dashed into the kitchen and tossed our metal lunch buckets on the counter, making a deafening clatter.

Mama was at the sink. "*Langsam!*" she laughed. "Slow down!"

I had forgotten. Before we could play, we had to show her our report cards. My parents were Germans, who immigrated to the U.S. in 1929 and went to night-school English class together. To them, getting an education, and doing well in school, were extremely important.

Carol and Sharon were first. They handed her their report cards at the same time. Mama dried her hands on her floral apron. She studied them for awhile. "*Wunderbar*," she said. "These are wonderful, girls." Carol was going into second grade and Sharon into first. They ran out, free and happy.

Willy handed his card to Mama. She looked at it. "Very good, Willy," she said. "*Sehr gut.*" He was going to be a sixth grader. He dashed happily off.

I stepped up and gave Mama my report card. She took a long time looking it over. I knew my grades were good and that I was going to be in Mrs. Nellis' fourth grade next year. But were they good enough for Mama?

Finally, she looked up at me, with a twinkle in her eye and a big smile on her face. She pinched my cheek lovingly and patted my head. I knew she was delighted. She pointed to the kitchen door. "Go," she said. "You play now, too!"

I bounded upstairs and changed from my school clothes to my vacation clothes— holey, faded jeans, a t-shirt, and old tennis shoes. Willy had already finished changing.

"Hey, Willy," I said. "Let's go fishing in the creek. We can keep cool that way."

"I have a better idea," he said. "You know how hot and sticky it gets in the summer. Let's make a swimming hole in the creek! It'll be our own private swimming pool!"

We dashed out. After several days of careful scouting, we found a likely place in the creek to make a swimming hole. The banks were high enough to hold lots of water. And there were shady trees on the shore. It was close to our house, just across our cow pasture and down a short trail.

The cow pasture, though, was surrounded by a barbed wire fence. "How will we get through?" I asked. "Piece o' cake," said Willy. "Just reach for the smooth wire between the barbs and pop the wire open."

That night, we told our sisters our plan. The next morning, we set out together. Willy popped the barbed wire open and held it so we could get through.

We ran to the creek, took off our shoes and socks, and rolled up our pants. To hold enough water for a swimming hole, we built a dam, using branches, dirt, rocks, and clumps of grass. We were playing Beaver! We worked all day long. It was hard, but fun. We were working for a common cause!

The next morning, we threw on our bathing suits and ran eagerly to the creek. But when we got there, our spirits sank. The dam was gone! The water had washed it away.

Willy was our Chief Engineer. He thought for a second. "We need more rocks," he said. "Bigger ones. And less dirt!" For the next few days, we gathered the biggest rocks and stones we could find. Then, we became Beavers again. We blocked the creek with our new, improved dam.

The next morning, we threw on our bathing suits and dashed back to the creek. We couldn't believe it. The dam had been washed away again! We trooped sadly back to the house and put our clothes back on. We sat there, trying to figure out what to do.

While we were thinking, Papa came in. "Why all the long faces?" he asked. We told him about our Beaver adventures.

That Saturday, Papa brought a posthole digger, hammer, saw, nails, wooden posts, and old barn boards to our spot. By sundown, we had a real dam. It even had a spillway to let some water continue flowing down the creek! He built a wooden supporting wall. We all stacked rocks behind it for added strength. No doubt about it, Papa was the Master Beaver!

On Sunday afternoon, we headed for our swimming hole. This time, we brought old towels and had our pants on over our swimming suits. We piled our clothes and towels in a clearing near the creek and jumped in. I took a deep breath, closed my eyes, held my nose shut, and dived. When I opened my eyes, the water looked gray and murky, not like in a swimming pool. But water is water, and it was wet and cool!

We tried lots of swimming styles, like the doggy-paddle, the Australian crawl, and the sidestroke. One day I was trying the backstroke when my hand touched something. It was a small turtle! I picked it up. It had a black bumpy shell, a pointed head with beady eyes, four legs with tiny needle-like claws, and a tail that moved quickly back and forth. It was a lot better than the wimpy pet turtle in my school classroom!

"Hey!" I yelled to my siblings. "Look at the turtle I caught!"

I held the turtle with one hand and tapped it gently, to see what it would do. OH! WOW! WHOA! HELP! It snapped onto my finger and wouldn't let go! I shook my arm as hard as I could, trying to shake it off. It worked! That snapper was now the world's first . . . Flying Teenage Ninja Turtle!

I looked at my hand. There was blood! We gathered our towels and clothes and headed home. As I got to the door, my hand started to hurt. "Mama!" I cried. "A turtle bit me! My finger's gonna fall off!!"

Mama took me into the bathroom. She gently washed my finger. Then, she opened the medicine cabinet and reached for a brown rectangular bottle with a medicine dropper in it. IODINE! I hated iodine. I knew it would hurt worse than the turtle bite!

She started filling the dropper. "Please," I pleaded. "Not iodine! It'll sting!" I squirmed, but she held me firmly. I looked away and gritted my teeth. This wasn't gonna be pleasant.

Using the glass rod, Mama applied a deep red liquid to my finger. I was getting ready to scream when I realized something. It didn't hurt! Mama smiled at me. "I found something new at the drug store," she said. "It's called Mercurochrome."

With a new white Band-Aid wrapped around my finger, Mama and I went into the kitchen. She gave me a big slice of her wonderful tomato soup cake. Its moistness and spicy flavor always comforted me. She made it with a can of tomato soup, and rich spices, raisins, and nuts. Then she sprinkled powered sugar over each piece. It was just the medicine I needed!

The next morning, Mama washed our swimming hole towels and clothes. From the cellar came the "whoosh whoosh" of the washing machine.

Suddenly, we heard a bloodcurdling scream. It was coming from the cellar! We all scrambled down the stairs. Mama was pointing into the washing machine.

"*Ansehen!*" She screamed. "See it *schwimm* in the *wasser*! Come *schnell!*" I looked in the washing machine. There, swimming in the soapy, sudsy water, was a turtle. I reached in with my healthy hand and grabbed it. It was the same one that had taken a piece out of me! It must have landed on our towels or clothes when I shook it off. In our hurry to get home, we must have accidentally carried it in.

I carried it upstairs and put it in the bathtub, with a little water. When Papa came home from work he said, "That's a snapping turtle! They have strong jaws and don't let go of anything. They can snap off a finger just like that!"

"Yeah," I said. "Thanks for telling me now!"

Papa shrugged. "At least something good can come out of this. We can make turtle soup. It's a fine delicacy that few people have tasted."

Turtle soup? All of us kids looked at each other and grimaced. Then we shouted in unison—"You can't make soup out of our turtle!"

Papa looked at us, then at the turtle. He wet his lips and rubbed his chin, as if in deep thought. He went behind the kitchen door and got the yardstick that was always there. Looking very serious, he measured the turtle. A grin played slowly over his face. "Oh, darn," he said. "It's too small to make into turtle soup!" He broke out laughing, as we kids cheered.

The next morning, we put the creature from the black swimming hole in a box. We threw it back in the creek, way downstream from our swimming hole.

On the way back, we saw that some cows were out of the pasture. We helped Papa get them back behind the barbed wire. "Guess those cows have seen you kids go through the fence so many times, they learned it from you," he joked. "I'll have to do something to keep them in."

Papa drove to the feed store in town. He came back with some rolls of smooth wire, and a big, bulky battery that had white, china-like things sticking out.

We were about to enter the Electric Fence Age. The white things were "insulators." Papa nailed two to each fence post. He went around the pasture twice, running the smooth wire around each insulator. Willy and I helped. He put the big battery in the barn and attached the wires from the fence to it.

Papa told us to stand back, then flipped a switch on the battery. It started making a strange sound—ZZZZNNANNZZZZ. Then, silence. Another ZZZZNNANNZZZZ. More silence. He said the battery had to have the electric charge continually go on (ZZZZNNANNZZZZ) and then off (silence) to keep its charge up.

Still, we had no problems getting to our swimming hole. Carol had great hearing. She told us when the fence was "hot" and when it wasn't. She figured there were seven seconds between on and off. When she said "Go!" we went!

The cows must have had the same skills, since they also just walked through the fence. So, back to the feed store went Papa. He returned with a small rectangular tin-like box with an electrical cord and a plug. Using that box, he connected the electric fence to the barn's electrical socket. Now the fence was "hot" full time. In fact, sometimes there were actual flames coming off the wires. That made our choice of a swimming hole spot not so hot! From then on, we kids walked the long way around the pasture fence to get to the swimming hole.

On Sunday nights, our family always watched Ed Sullivan's "Toast of the Town" on our 17-inch black-and-white Raytheon TV. One night we saw a troupe of tumblers. They flew over each other, and over and through this and that. For their finale, they jumped through hoops of fire.

We kids looked at each other. Light bulbs went on over our heads! We had all thought of the same plan.

The next morning, we went to the soft part of the hay mow and imitated the tumblers. Dive, tuck, and roll! After many miscues and hard landings, we were expert tumblers. After a few more days of practice, we were ready for our finale—diving through the "hoops of fire" on the electric fence. It would be easy. Just dive, tuck, and roll between the wires!

I could just see us on Ed Sullivan. "And now," he'd say, "The Ruby Tumbling Kids." As I got ready for my dive, Willy made drum roll sounds. I did my best dive, tuck, and roll. Next thing I knew, I was on the other side of the fence, in the pasture. From then on, it was easy to get to our swimming hole. Dive, tuck, and roll! (Something the cows never figured out, for some reason.)

One day we had visitors. Judy Schmelsley, the girl of my dreams, the girl I had a secret crush on, came with her parents. Now, I could impress her with my tumbling skills. I just had to do the usual dive, tuck, and roll!

When my chance came, I was a little nervous. After this shining act of bravery, Judy would be in love with me forever! I started running. Willy wasn't there, so I did my own drum roll.

It was dive, tuck, and SQUISH! All of a sudden, I was flat on my back. I noticed a strong, earthy odor around me. I had slipped on a large, fresh, still warm cow patty— and had landed on it!

I got up slowly and took off my shirt. All I could hear was laughter! I wanted to hold my nose. I saw Judy heading back to the house, laughing. She'd probably tell everyone what had happened. Off I went to the swimming hole. If I put this shirt into the wash, Mama would be screaming again. I went downstream to where we let the turtle go and rinsed off almost every piece of cow pie.

Too soon, it was Labor Day! School was about to start! Now, it was more school, more books, more teacher's dirty looks. My first day in fourth grade started with a bus ride with Mr. Duell at the wheel of his brand new, shining orange bus #24!

As we headed to school, I looked back over the summer. I realized I hadn't stopped learning when I got off Old 8 a few months ago. School was a good place to learn, but a one-hundred acre farm was also a great learning place. Why, it had been a perfect classroom for:

Teamwork
Keeping on task
Practicing skills
Thinking about new ways to do things
Knowing about nature
Learning from mistakes
Problem solving
Planning
. . . and more!

I knew I'd learn a lot from Mrs. Nellis. But I also knew I'd learn by just living on our spacious farm with my parents, brother, and sisters. Learning was all around me—I just had to keep my mind open.

Glossary:

Ansehen!	Look at that!
Langsam!	Slow down!
Schnell	Fast, quickly
Schwimm	Swim
Sehr gut	Very good
Wasser	Water
Wunderbar	Wonderful, marvelous

Mama Ruby's Tomato Soup Cake
(Serves 12-14)

1/2 cup shortening
1 cup sugar
1 can tomato soup (undiluted – right
    from the can)
2 eggs
2 cups flour
2 teaspoons baking powder
1/2 teaspoon baking soda

1-1/2 teaspoons cinnamon
1-1/2 teaspoons nutmeg
1/2 teaspoon cloves
1/2 teaspoon allspice
1/2 cup raisins
1/2 cup nuts (optional, but Mama always
    used walnuts)

1. Preheat oven to 350 degrees.
2. In a medium bowl, cream the shortening and the sugar.
3. Add soup right out of the can. Do not add any water. Mix.
4. Add the eggs and mix thoroughly.
5. In another bowl, sift together the flour, baking soda, baking powder, and spices. Add to first mixture.
6. Beat combined mixture until smooth. Add raisins and nuts (optional).
7. Bake in a 9 X 9 inch pan or an 8 X 10 inch pan at 350 degrees until done, about 25-30 minutes.
8. Cool.

Before serving, dust with confectionery sugar.

Sometimes Mama would surprise us and substitute a 6-oz. package of chocolate chips for the raisins and nuts.

Mama Ruby's Homemade Tomato Noodle Soup
(Serves 4)

When we had an overabundant tomato harvest, Mama made her own tomato juice and would use it in this recipe. Regular store-bought canned tomato juice also works great.

4 tablespoons butter
2 tablespoons flour
4 cups tomato juice
1 cup water

1/4 cup sugar
1/4 teaspoon salt
1 or 2 cups cooked wide egg noodles

1. In a two-quart saucepan, melt the butter. Add the flour, and stir to form a smooth paste.
2. Slowly add the tomato juice and water. Stir continuously to boiling.
3. Cook for two minutes or until thickened, then add the sugar and salt.
4. Stir in the noodles and heat until noodles are hot.

Pig's Ears! Yuck!

© 2005 Kathryn Beisner

by Kathryn Beisner

"Pig's ears! Yuck!" I said when Mom told me about the special recipe that Grandma was making just for our visit.

"You'll like them," she said with a grin.

I knew better than to sass Mom and say "No I won't!" But that's what I was thinking. Pig's ears sounded gross, like that *studenina* thing made with pig's feet. It looked like the hooves were hanging in clear Jell-O. "I'm gonna gag," I thought, so I rolled down the car window.

Our whole family was in the car, a white four-door sedan. It was brand new, and we four girls had to keep it clean, or else. We didn't really know what "or else" was, but when Dad said it in his Air Force voice, we knew better than to find out.

My sister Gretchen was seven years older than me and had just graduated from high school. At fourteen, Carolyn was only two-and-a-half years older than me. But I was older than Janine. She was only going into the first grade next year.

Mom and Dad sat up front. Carolyn sat between them because she threw up if she sat in the back seat. I sat behind Dad until Gretchen or Janine said it was their turn to sit next to the window. Then I took my spot on the floor. I was just the right size to lie on my back on one side of the hump and put my feet on the other side. I liked it there because the vibration and hum of the tires drowned out what everyone else was saying and made it seem like I was all by myself. My sisters were glad to put their stocking feet up on the back seat, without getting into trouble.

We were a military family. Whenever anyone found out my dad was in the Air Force, they'd say to me, "Oh, you're a military brat!" But they would be smiling, so I hoped it was just a joke, even though I didn't think it was very funny.

Dad had been in the Army Air Corps during World War II, before any of us girls were born. The Air Corps was the part of the U.S. Army devoted to combat in the sky. But when the war was over, that part of the Army became its own branch of the military. Since 1947 it has been called the United States Air Force.

Being a military family meant that we moved to wherever the Air Force needed my dad at the time. But the Air Force never needed my dad in Pennsylvania, which was where Grandma and Grandpa lived. We didn't get to be with our grandparents very often, so it was a fun time when we took a road trip to see them. And that's where we were going now!

That morning, we had left the air base in Louisiana where we currently lived. Usually we visited Grandma and Grandpa in the summer, when we were out of school. But this was a special occasion, so we were traveling in January.

Believe it or not, we were going to celebrate Christmas, again! And we were going to get presents again, too!

Mom called it "Grandma's Christmas." Grandma called it "The Feast of the Three Kings." But really it's Christmas for all of the Orthodox and Eastern rite churches. Those churches use the Julian calendar instead of the one we're used to, the Gregorian calendar. The 13-day difference between them happened almost 500 years ago, but I didn't care about that. I just knew that we were going to have two Christmases this year!

I also knew that when we got there, Grandma would be making traditional Ukrainian recipes to celebrate the day. Some of her traditional foods were delicious, like *pyrohy*. All of the recipes that Grandma made had strange-sounding names, like *holubtsi* and *borsch*.

The names didn't scare me, though. Our family had traveled all around the United States, and even to Europe. We ate lots of foods that other people considered to be different, like corn fritters in Texas, Camembert cheese in France, and Rocky Mountain oysters in Colorado.

As Dad drove us through Tennessee and Kentucky on the second day of our trip, I thought about when my mom had placed studenina in front of me the first time. Anybody could tell they were jellied pig's feet! Yuck! I couldn't even look at them, let alone eat them. Now she was talking about pig's ears! All I could think about was another big pot of disgusting animal parts in boiling water.

Long ago many Ukrainians were poor, so they developed a tradition of being frugal. That meant they didn't waste anything, including food. Once an animal was killed, they ate as much of it as they could. So they created recipes that used the feet, and even the tongue.

I liked learning about my Ukrainian heritage, what the customs were, and how they came to be important. One of my favorite traditions was egg decorating, called *pysanka*. The egg is a symbol of eternal life in the Ukrainian Catholic Church, so people created beautiful egg designs as a celebration of their religious beliefs.

Grandma had designed and hand decorated her own eggs for many years. They were the most interesting eggs I had ever seen. At Easter, our family usually dipped each egg in one color, and that was it. But Grandma didn't dip the eggs. She carefully applied wax and dye to them. And each one had many colors, such as dark blue, reddish purple, yellow, pink, orange, red, and even white. The lines of color on Grandma's eggs created a detailed pattern of age-old symbols from her village in Ukraine.

Mom had some eggs that Grandma had decorated especially for her, years ago. They felt light as air because the insides had evaporated. All that was left were the thin eggshells, so they were very fragile. They could easily break if they were handled roughly, so each one was wrapped in a Kleenex® and put in an old egg carton for safekeeping. In the spring, Mom would gently place the eggs in a glass bowl filled with green Easter grass. We weren't allowed to touch them. But when Mom wasn't looking, my sisters and I would see who could get her face closest to the bowl without leaving a nose print.

We finally got to Grandma and Grandpa's house on the third day of our trip. I was excited about celebrating a second Christmas. But I was getting nervous about having to face another recipe made from leftover parts of a pig. I was hoping that Mom would forget about the pig's ears, or that there were no pigs left in Pennsylvania for Grandma to cook with!

We got out of the car in front of the little house, and Grandma came out onto the porch to meet us. I hung back a little, trying to make myself invisible, but Grandma called out, "Kada," my Ukrainian nickname. She hugged me with her strong arms, and I noticed that now I was almost as tall as she was.

With a thick Ukrainian accent, she said in broken English, "For you, I make pig's ears, like you mother say. Come, come." Grandma took my hand and led me in the front door, through the living room and dining room, and into the tiny kitchen.

I'd been dreading this moment for three days. Nervously, I squished my eyes into tiny slits, so I wouldn't be able to see very well. I could make out the big, cast iron skillet bubbling with oil. Off to one side of the stove, I could kind of see a piece of cloth lined with rows of something golden brown and squiggly looking.

"That's them," I thought. I couldn't help myself. I blurted out, "YUCK! Pig's ears!"

Then, I noticed there was a sweet aroma in the kitchen, not at all like the smell of meat cooking. I opened my eyes and saw Grandma's kneading board holding several strips of flat dough. It wasn't what I had expected.

Confused, I looked at Grandma. She had a broad smile on her face. Then I heard laughing. I looked around to see that Mom and Dad, my sisters, Grandpa, Uncle Moxie, and Aunt Ann were all standing around smiling, looking at my expression.

What Grandma had made was *khrusty*, one of the twelve courses in the traditional Ukrainian Christmas Eve supper. Khrusty are made from pastry dough that has been sliced into strips. A slit is cut into the middle of each strip, and one end of the strip is pulled through the opening to form a loose loop. Each loop is fried in oil until it puffs up and turns golden brown. That makes them look like pointy, bent pig's ears! They got their name from how they look, not from their ingredients!

Mom turned to me. "Grandma really got you this time," she said, and everybody laughed again. I felt my face getting hot with embarrassment because I realized I had been the latest target of Grandma's famous sense of humor. But Grandma gave me a warm hug, and then I laughed, too.

"You like, now you make," said Grandma with a smile. She gestured to the dough, inviting me to help her make more khrustys. After Grandma showed me what to do, I pulled the ends through the slits of each of the doughy pieces on her kneading board. She had saved them to do with me, because she knew how much I liked to cook with her. Carefully, I slid each loop into the hot oil, and Grandma scooped them out when they were done.

For the last step, I got to sprinkle a little bit of powdered sugar on the brown, crispy pig's ears. Now, I looked forward to tasting the food I had been dreading for the last three days. I bit into the crunchy pastry and said, "Oh, Grandma, these are great!" There was nothing but air inside them, and the fried, crusty dough melted quickly in my mouth. I reached for another, and then Grandma let me have a third one, too. We laughed together again at the idea of eating the real ears off of pigs. Yuck!

The next day was Grandma's Christmas, and my sisters and I got to open presents for the second time in two weeks! I really liked my gifts, like the wooden lawn ornament that Uncle Moxie made for me. It was a duck with wings that spun around faster and faster as the wind blew through them. But the best present of all was feeling close to Grandma as I helped her make khrustys.

18

That week with Grandma and Grandpa went by fast. Soon, I was on the floor of the back seat again, as Dad drove us back home. Down there, in my own private world, I thought about how special our visit had been. Actually, all of our trips to Pennsylvania seemed special. I guessed it was because they were always planned around holidays, when Grandma made traditional foods that we didn't get every day. Then, all year long, we told stories about those wonderful meals, as we remembered the tastes and smells of our Ukrainian heritage.

We weren't even home yet, but I was already thinking about our next trip. When Grandma had hugged me goodbye, she said that when we visited the next time, she would make pigs-in-a-blanket!

Glossary:

Borsch	The national soup of Ukraine, made with beets
Holubtsi	Cabbage rolls filled with rice and buckwheat
Khrusty	Deep-fried pastry dough that looks like pig's ears
Pyrohy	Triangle-shaped dumplings filled with potatoes and onions
Pysanka	Egg decoration using traditional Ukrainian designs
Studenina	Jellied pig's feet

Grandma's "Pig's Ears"
(Khrusty)

2 eggs
4 cups flour
1 teaspoon baking powder
2/3 teaspoon salt
1/3 cup butter
1/2 cup sugar
Water to work dough

Beat eggs well. Add remaining ingredients; mix. Knead on floured board until smooth. Cover dough with cloth; set aside for 1 to 2 hours. Roll dough to 1/8 inch thick, a small amount of dough at a time. Cut dough into long strips about 1-1/4 inches wide. Cut strips into 3-inch lengths. Slit each piece in the center, pulling one end through to form a loose loop. Cover to prevent drying. Deep fry in oil or shortening at 350 degrees until both sides are golden brown. Drain on paper towels. When cool, dust with confectioner's sugar.

Aunt Lorraine's Mandelbrot Comes to Denver

by Steve Lee

This is a story about rediscovering family roots, and eating. It's not about eating roots.

My family is from the Chicago area. My parents lived in a high-rise apartment building in downtown Chicago. But when I was born in 1951, they bought a home in Park Forest, which was about 30 miles away. It was a new area that was considered an innovation in housing—a "suburb." That was short for "sub-urban area."

In downtown Chicago, everyone lived in big apartment buildings. The only grass was in parks, and no one had their own driveway. When my friends and I wanted to play outside, we had to go to a parking lot, or to a park. But in our new suburb, people lived in their own houses. They had their own lawns, and their own driveways. My dad could park right in his driveway, and my friends and I could play outside our own houses.

The city could be an unfriendly place. But in Park Forest, neighbors watched out for each other. We kids played outside until dark, when the fireflies would appear, blinking on and off in the night. Our dads would sit on the front porches and discuss the home improvement projects they planned for their houses. Stores like Home Depot didn't exist back then, but we had a neighborhood hardware store that sold everything you could want for making home improvements. I think my dad would have moved to Park Forest just to be able to have his own house that he could work on!

Much later, when I was older and went to college, I read about the development of suburbs in America. Sure enough, one of my sociology textbooks discussed my suburb, Park Forest, Illinois, as an innovation in housing that is now the way most Americans live.

Our little house in Park Forest had two bedrooms, a living room, a kitchen, and a bathroom. There was no basement or garage. But it had a great place that we called the "utility room." That's where all the cool mechanical stuff was: the furnace, the washing machine, the clothes dryer, and the water heater. We didn't have our own washer and dryer when we lived in an apartment in Chicago. My mother was happy with this new arrangement. What a convenience—she could do the wash right at home!

I liked the washer and dryer for another reason. They were noisy! I even figured out a way to make the washer noisier. In those days, there was no safety switch on the lid of the washer. When you opened the lid, the machine kept running. One day, I waited until the machine was in the "spin" cycle. Then, I held a piece of stiff wire against the center agitator! Man, what a great racket! At least, until my mother marched in.

"Steven!" she yelled. (She only called me by my full name when she was really mad!) "Don't you know how dangerous that is! Your Aunt Lorraine's neighbor's sister's boy had his arm ripped off by a washing machine just last week! Get away from that thing!"

I didn't know that Aunt Lorraine had a neighbor who had a sister, or that the neighbor's sister had a son. I had my doubts about the story that some kid got his arm ripped off, but I didn't argue. I just made sure that the next time I put the wire in the washing machine, I didn't make as much racket.

Another great new thing about living in Park Forest was something I had never seen before—a supermarket! Everything that a family could possibly eat was under one roof. I wasn't all that impressed with it, but my parents were awestruck. When they grew up, you had to go to a different kind of store for each type of food. If you wanted meat, you went to the meat market. If you wanted bread, you went to the bakery. Going to the supermarket was much quicker and easier. No wonder my parents liked it!

But there was one thing about the supermarket that my parents didn't like. It didn't have the special foods that my family ate. We were Jewish, and we followed the "kosher" laws, which say what you can and can't eat. Even though it seemed to have everything else, the supermarket didn't have kosher foods.

So we had to go to stores that had kosher foods. Some of them were my absolute favorites—like cold beet borsch (a kind of soup) served with sour cream. And gefilte fish (which was really sturgeon, but I didn't care). I also loved lox (smoked salmon) and bagels.

But my favorite food of all was (and still is) Mandelbrot. It's a special cake-like cookie that you can eat by itself, but which is absolutely great with a glass of cold milk! I can remember eating Mandelbrot and drinking milk until I couldn't hold another bite! It was crunchy, but not too hard. Chewy, but not sticky. Flavorful, but not overpowering. It was the best dessert ever. Sometimes, I even had Mandelbrot for breakfast!

In our family, Aunt Lorraine, who still lived in Chicago, was the one who made Mandelbrot. Oh, how I loved traveling back to the city to Aunt Lorraine's house. I always knew there would be Mandelbrot waiting for me!

The years passed, though, and things changed. Sadly, my parents divorced, and I moved to Denver, away from my Chicago (and Park Forest) roots. I didn't see my dad's family very much. I especially missed Aunt Lorraine—and her Mandelbrot.

As I grew older, I graduated from college. I met a wonderful woman, and Lynette, bless her heart, agreed to marry me. Like all married couples, one of the things we talked about was our favorite foods. Hers seemed pretty tame—okay, but not very interesting. One of them was her mother's homemade bread. When she was growing up, her mother would fry it in hot oil. Another family favorite was "monkey bread," but that's another story!

I love Lynette, but since she's not Jewish, she wasn't used to Jewish foods. For her, the cold beet borscht that I love, served with sour cream, seemed very strange. She thought it was awful! But at least, she put up with my eating it. Not so with gefilte fish. For her, it was just an unidentifiable white fishy mass. She took one look at it and told me to forget it. She wouldn't even try it. When I ate it, she said my breath smelled like cat food.

But I'm happy to say that when I told her about Mandelbrot, she said she might like it. She thought it might be great for dunking in coffee. I told her it should only be dunked in milk, never in coffee. But I was still pleased that she said she might like it.

The only problem was that I didn't have a recipe for it! The one who had the recipe was our family's official Mandelbrot maker, Aunt Lorraine. I knew that the next time we went to Chicago to visit, Lynette would finally experience the most delightful cookie in the world—and that Aunt Lorraine would give us the recipe.

On our next visit to Chicago, Aunt Lorraine made us feel right at home. She told me lots of family stories that I had never heard, mostly about my father. Sometimes Aunt Lorraine and my father disagreed about the details of those stories. They even disagreed on the proper spelling for Mandelbrot! My dad spells it "Mandelbroht." But since Aunt Lorraine gave me the recipe, I follow her spelling. My dad always rolls his eyes when he sees how Aunt Lorraine spells it. But they always laugh off their disagreements, instead of getting angry.

Unfortunately, on that visit, Aunt Lorraine couldn't give me her recipe for Mandelbrot. She hadn't used the recipe for awhile, and she couldn't remember where she had put it. She said she'd send it as soon as she could. Oh, how I looked forward to getting that recipe in the mail from Chicago!

Soon after we got home, a letter arrived from Aunt Lorraine. Tucked in the envelope was an index card with the Mandelbrot recipe. I felt like a kid on Christmas (actually, Chanukah) morning! I quickly scanned the list of ingredients to see if we had everything we needed to cook up a batch. Agony! It would take a trip to the supermarket. But at least we could do all our shopping in one store! We wouldn't have to go to the dairy store for milk, eggs, and butter, then to the dry goods store for flour, sugar, and nuts. In no time at all, we'd be eating Mandelbrot!

When we got home, Lynette laid out the ingredients, while I read the recipe card over and over. I wanted to make sure we followed the instructions carefully. Everything had to be measured, then blended just so. This was Mandelbrot. It had to be right!

With high hopes, we started following the recipe. But soon, it became apparent something was wrong. Our old electric mixer was bogging down in the thick Mandelbrot mixture. We figured that we must have misread the recipe and forgotten to add some liquid. But no. We had done everything according to the directions. I called Aunt Lorraine in Chicago. She confirmed that the Mandelbrot batter should be like bread dough. But our electric mixer just sputtered and died.

Lynette rolled her eyes. "Your Mandel-whatever-you-call-it just ate my mixer!" She handed me a large kitchen spoon. "If you want it," she warned, "you're gonna have to mix it by hand." I rolled up my sleeves and mixed the batter. I was determined to have Mandelbrot tonight!

Before long, our little kitchen was filled with the most wonderful smell in the world. My mind was back in Chicago in the 1950s. My mouth was watering for a taste of fresh-from-the-oven Mandelbrot! Ahhh! When it came out of the oven, it was every bit as good as I had remembered. Even Lynette liked it!

Soon afterward, Aunt Lorraine came for a visit. And she brought a box filled with Mandelbrot! Inside the box, separated by sheets of silver foil, were layers upon layers of Mandelbrot. What a delightful gift!

But wait. This Mandelbrot was different. It had slivered almonds, like the Mandelbrot that I remembered. And the color was right—lightly toasted. But some of the pieces had chocolate chips in them! And some had walnuts! What? The time-honored recipe had been modified! The traditional cookie had been changed! How could she have done this?

Aunt Lorraine saw the look on my face. She gazed at me over the top of her glasses and sighed. "Gimme a break!" she said. "I think they taste great with chocolate chips!" She looked at my wife. "Don't you agree, Lynette?"

My wife picked up a piece of Mandelbrot. She dipped it in a cup of coffee and smiled at me. "The chips make your aunt's Mandelbrot absolutely perfect," she said. "Don't you agree, Steve?"

So much for tradition . . . .

Aunt Lorraine's Mandelbrot

1. In a large mixing bowl, cream together the following ingredients, using an electric mixer:

   1 stick butter or margarine
   3 tablespoons cooking oil
      (NOT olive oil!)
   1 cup sugar

   1/2 teaspoon vanilla
   1/2 teaspoon almond flavoring
   1 tablespoon lemon juice

2. In a separate bowl, mix together the following ingredients. Don't add the above mixture yet.

   3 cups flour
   1 teaspoon baking powder

   1 teaspoon baking soda
   1/2 teaspoon salt

3. Beat three eggs well. Add a small amount of the beaten eggs to the creamed butter or margarine mixture. Mix, then add a small amount of the flour mixture. Mix again.
4. Alternate adding eggs and flour until all ingredients are mixed. The resulting dough will be very thick.
5. Add one cup of sliced almonds (or walnuts), and mix. If you wish, add (heavy sigh) chocolate chips. What the heck! Go for it, and put all three in!

Cowboy Days

by David Henley

"Time to get up, cowboys!"

The deep voice boomed from across the room as I lay in my hard bunk. I opened my eyes to see who it was. I had to blink. I had forgotten how bright the sun could be at 6:45 in the morning.

The voice went on. "Get your boots on, and don't forget your cowboy hats. See you outside in twenty minutes for breakfast."

That was Cowboy Bob. He had welcomed us to the Bar None Ranch in Idaho the night before. He was five foot nine, muscular, with a thick salt-and-pepper mustache. He had been a cowboy all his life.

I was in the bunkhouse with seven other boys who had come for a "cowboy experience." I had always been fascinated by cowboys. I had seen all of Clint Eastwood's westerns. And I never missed an episode of "Texas Rangers." Now, at thirteen, I had persuaded my mother to let me come to the Bar None. I had come out with my cousin, Tony, who was fifteen.

"Hey, Tony," I said as we got dressed. "Why do we have to get started so early?"

"Thought you knew," he said. "We don't want to be on the trail when it gets hot." He looked at me. "How many times you say you've been riding?"

"Just once," I said. I paused for effect. "But I think I'm a natural. Ain't nothing they can toss my way that I can't handle." Tony looked doubtful.

"Okay, hotshot," I said. "How many times have you been on a horse?"

"A couple of times. Once at that lodge in upstate New York. And a couple of summers ago at camp. But I know I've got plenty to learn."

"Don't worry," I said. "I hear all they have here is old mares that walk real slow." I nudged him with my elbow. Actually, I was anxious about riding, but I didn't want him to know.

We finished getting ready and headed out. Some of the boys were standing by a long wooden table. Cowboys in off-white aprons were setting out big bowls and platters of food.

"Gather round for roll call," yelled Cowboy Bob. He called the roll, starting with "Cowboy Mark" and ending with "Cowboy Aaron."

"Okay," he said. "We'll do this each day before breakfast and after supper. Gotta make sure we don't lose any cowpokes out on the trail."

"And just so you know," he added, "We get up at 5:30 from now on. I let you sleep in your first day."

Tony and I looked at each other. Lost cowpokes? Up at 5:30? Why hadn't they told us that before we came?

"Okay," said Cowboy Bob. "After breakfast, meet me at the stable for our first ride." He pointed to a large building that looked like a barn.

I wondered if I was the only one wondering what the difference was between a barn and a stable.

"And if you're thinkin' of bringin' a snack, don't. Last thing I need's a cowpoke ridin' with one hand, eatin' with the other, and fallin' off his horse!"

The chow bell rang. We all sat down. As I reached for some eggs, Cowboy Bob held out his hand. "A prayer before we start," he said. That was something I could relate to. We always did that at home.

"Yup," he said. "Ever since that ol' bear attacked me here three years ago, been sayin' a prayer 'fore I go out on a ride." He paused. "Dear Father, we thank you for another beautiful day on the Bar None, and for this great spread o' food. We ask You to watch over us on our ride. Amen."

When the prayer ended, I was picturing bears lurking along the trail. But even that couldn't spoil my appetite. There were eggs, bacon, sausage, biscuits, grits, oatmeal, orange juice, and milk. Everyone else was hungry, too. All you could hear was the clanking of the silverware. In ten minutes, we were all done.

I got up with Tony and headed toward the stable. "Oh," I said. "I almost forgot."

I ran back to the bunkhouse and got a package that my mom had given me. I caught up to Tony by the stable.

"What's that?" he asked.

"Apple crisp squares that Mom made. Gonna take 'em with me."

"You kidding? Cowboy Bob said not to bring anything."

"It's okay. Anyway, after that big breakfast, I probably won't get hungry."

Just then, Cowboy Bob walked up. "You're Cowboy Darius and Cowboy Tony, right?"

"Yes, sir," I said proudly.

"You'll like this ride. It's real scenic up by Crawford Lake. Usually see some deer or elk." He looked around. "Since you two got here first, you can have your pick o' horses. Come on."

The stable had about twenty horses. We examined them closely. I had heard that a good horse could make a ride much easier. I wished I knew how to spot one.

After awhile, Tony stopped. He pointed to a big black horse with rippling muscles. "I want this one," he said.

"That's Rudy," said Cowboy Bob. "Always wants to be up front, so we made him our lead horse." He looked at Tony. "Make sure you let him know you're in charge. Cowboy Bill will get you set up." Tony headed outside.

"Cowboy Bob?" I said.

"Yes, Cowboy Darius?"

"How do you pick a horse? I mean, a really good one?"

"Aww, I don't know if there's any kinda method. You and the horse'll just know you're right for each other."

We kept walking through the stable. About halfway through, I got a funny feeling. I turned around. A horse was looking my way. I could have sworn it looked me up and down and then looked me right in the eye. It felt kind of weird, but it also felt comforting.

"Cowboy Bob," I said. "Can I ride that horse? The red one with the white spot on his face?"

"Guess so. But it's chestnut, not red. And it's a she, not a he." He paused. "That's Daisy. Good choice. Been here the longest, and she's real gentle."

"Okay, I choose Daisy."

"Looks like she already chose you. Come on. I'll get you saddled up."

By that time, the other boys had arrived and were picking their horses. Cowboy Bob grabbed a saddle and put it on Daisy. He led her outside and told me to get on.

I went to Daisy's right side and started to climb on.

"Come around to the left," said Cowboy Bob. "Always mount a horse on the left side. I'll give you a leg up."

Tony was already on his horse, looking at me. "I knew you mount on the left," I said, looking at him. "Just got a little confused." Tony made a face as Cowboy Bob helped me up.

We waited while the other kids mounted their horses. "Okay, cowpokes," yelled Cowboy Bob. "Are any of you expert riders?"

I shot my hand up and looked around. No other hands were up, not even Tony's.

I turned toward Cowboy Bob. "Guess you and me are the only experienced riders," I said proudly.

"Okay," he said. "We'll just have to look after the rest of these cowboys."

I turned and grinned at Tony. He rolled his eyes.

"Listen up," said Cowboy Bob. "Before we get goin', I gotta give you cowpokes a few instructions."

He showed us how to kick with both legs to get our horse started, how to use the reins to steer the horse left or right, and how to stop. We practiced until he felt sure we all knew the basics. He showed us how to get down and then back up again.

"Now," he said, "let's get lined up. Cowboy Tony'll take the lead, on Rudy. I'll ride alongside him. The rest of you'll be behind us. Cowboy Darius'll be at the end, on Daisy. He'll see if anyone gets in trouble. If you do, he'll help you out. Right, Cowboy Darius?"

I breathed hard. "Right," I said, trying to sound confident.

"Okay," he yelled. "Let's go!"

We headed out the gate, under the Bar None Ranch sign, across the field, and over a hill. It was a good start. We went through a meadow, then through a clump of white pine trees. In the distance, I saw just what I had hoped to see—a group of elk. They were magnificent!

We went on through the pine trees, ducking under low branches. Only a few rays of sunlight were making it through the trees. It was cool and damp. I saw two ground squirrels, one chasing the other around a tree. Birds were calling to each other. It was what I had been waiting for those many months. Everything felt calm and peaceful. This ride was gonna be a piece of cake!

After awhile, we reached a stream. "Okay, cowpokes," said Cowboy Bob. "Let's give those horses a well-deserved drink!"

We all got down. I got my foot caught in the stirrup and almost fell. I looked around. Whew! Except for Daisy, nobody had noticed. She headed straight for what seemed to be her favorite spot. She started to drink and then stopped. She turned and looked straight at me with her big brown eyes. I knew she was asking if I was okay.

I walked over to her. "I'm fine, girl," I said softly as I patted her neck. "Go ahead and drink."

While the horses drank, we enjoyed the scenery. Cowboy Bob told us about the trees and bushes around us. He told us how to identify the fish in the stream. I was in Cowboy Heaven!

After ten minutes, it was time to go. We mounted up. Cowboy Bob said he'd cross the stream first, then Tony, then everyone else. As before, I was in the back.

Just as I was easing Daisy into the stream, I saw something at the water's edge, further down the trail. It looked like a moose. "I'll take a look," I thought. "I'll be back before anyone misses me." I made sure I remembered where to cross the stream, then headed over. But I guess even a cowboy doesn't always see things right. It was just a bunch of big branches that had fallen in the stream.

"Come on, girl," I said to Daisy. "We gotta catch up." By the time I made it back to the crossing point, almost everyone else was already across. I guided Daisy into the stream.

I prodded Daisy to go fast, so we could catch up before anyone noticed. About midway across, I saw a school of trout to my right. I wanted to look. I leaned over to the right and pulled hard for Daisy to stop. Bad idea. Between the sudden stop and my leaning over, I lost my balance.

"Hey," I yelled.

As I fell in, the force of the water flipped me upside down, then right side up again. When I got my head back above the water, Daisy was on the other side of the stream.

I yelled as the water pulled me under again. This time, when I came up, I couldn't see Daisy. I started to panic. Suddenly, I felt a tug at the back of my shirt. I was being pulled up. After the third tug, I was out of the water. I lay on the river bank, trying to catch my breath.

I looked to see who had saved me. Cowboy Bob, I thought, or maybe Cousin Tony. To my surprise, all I could see was Daisy's backside. She was ignoring me completely. At first I couldn't tell what she was doing. Then, I realized— she was eating my apple crisp! It must have fallen out of my sack when I collapsed on the bank.

I heard the sound of hoofbeats. It was the other cowboys, and Cowboy Bob. I grabbed the apple crisp from Daisy, put it behind my back, and turned around.

"You okay?" Cowboy Bob asked in a concerned voice.

I looked up. I was embarrassed that I had pretended to be an experienced rider and had ended up being the only cowboy to have a problem. But I couldn't show it in front of the other boys. Especially not in front of Tony, who looked like he was trying hard not to laugh.

"Yup," I said as I jumped, dripping, to my feet. "Never been better!"

Cowboy Bob smiled. "Well, Cowboy Darius, I saw how Daisy here pulled you out. Guess she was really lookin' out for you."

He looked at the sun to gauge the time. "Well," he said, "it's gettin' late. We better head on back and get you some dry clothes." He turned to the other boys. "That okay with you, cowpokes?"

There was some grumbling, but not a lot. "Yeah," said Tony. "I wouldn't feel safe without our most experienced rider at a hundred percent." I could see the smirk on his face as he said that, but I let it be.

That evening, before dinner, I walked to the stable. I wanted to thank Daisy for saving my life. I went to her stall. She was lying on the hay.

"Hi Daisy," I said. She looked up at me. She didn't seem too friendly.

"How are you, girl?" I asked. She made a grunting sound.

"I just wanted to thank you for saving my life today. And to say that I want you to be my horse for all the rides."

If she was impressed, she didn't show it.

"I brought you something," I said, reaching into a bag I was carrying. "Another piece of my mom's double cinnamon apple crisp. Just don't tell any of the other horses, okay?"

Daisy stood up. She trotted over and started to eat right out of my hand. The apple crisp was gone in three bites.

"I know why you like my mom's apple crisp," I said. "You like it 'cause its sweet, like you."

She still didn't react. I figured it was only the apple crisp that she liked, not me. I turned around and headed back toward the bunkhouse.

When I had taken a few steps, I heard a loud "neighhhhh." I turned around.

Daisy nodded several times. She stuck her head over the wall of her stall. Then she nodded again.

I walked over. I patted her head and stroked her neck. She neighed happily. I stayed with her for a few more minutes. It was just me and Daisy. Nothing else mattered.

I heard the dinner bell ring. I knew it was time to get back to camp. As I headed back, a thought hit me. I realized that Cowboy Bob had been right. Daisy and I were meant for each other, after all.

Daisy's Double Cinnamon Apple Crisp

1. Place 3-1/2 cups of apple slices in a buttered 13 X 9 inch pan.
2. Sprinkle with 2 teaspoons cinnamon and 1/2 teaspoon salt.
3. Add 1/4 cup water.
4. Rub together 3/4 cup flour, 1 cup brown sugar, and 1/3 cup butter.
5. Drop mixture over apples.
6. Bake at 350 degrees for 40 minutes.

Little Shawney and the Doughnut Disaster

by Virginia Fox

Johnny was born and raised in a little coal-mining town in Pennsylvania. The name of the town was Freeland. Most of the people who lived in this town were not born in the United States. They had come from many different countries, hoping to find a better life. Johnny's grandfather came from Germany.

Because they grew up speaking a different language, the older people in the town sometimes had trouble pronouncing English words. Many of them called Johnny "Little Shawney" (their way of pronouncing "Johnny").

Little Shawney's father was the town baker. He owned and operated a German bakery. The people in Freeland enjoyed their different ethnic customs and foods, but they all agreed on one thing—Little Shawney's father made the best doughnuts they had ever tasted.

In Freeland, people strictly observed the Lenten season (which comes before Easter). Everyone gave up something for Lent that they especially enjoyed. Usually it was sweet treats. More often than not, it was the delicious doughnuts that Little Shawney's father made.

The day before Lent was known in Freeland as Fastnacht (Fast Night). It was the day before the Fast started. On that day, people would usually eat great quantities of the treat they were giving up for Lent, since they would not have it for some time to come.

37

One particular Lent, Little Shawney was eight years old and his brother Irving was sixteen. Shawney looked up to his brother; he wanted to be just like him. He was already like him in one way; he had bright red hair, just like Irving. But he also wanted to be tall and smart like his brother. Their older sister, Elizabeth, was away at Nursing School. Sadly, their mother had died three years before. A housekeeper named Mary came and looked after them during the day. She also helped out Shawney's father by doing the cooking and cleaning.

Irving worked in his father's bakery, which had tables and chairs where you could sit down and have a cup of coffee with your doughnuts and pastry.

Little Shawney was too young to work at the bakery, but sometimes he helped when Papa needed an extra hand. He did chores like filling the cream puffs and putting sugar on the doughnuts. He loved helping, because this gave him a chance to be with his papa.

As Fastnacht Day approached, Shawney's father knew that he would need to have mountains of doughnuts ready. The night before, he started early; mixing, cutting, frying. He worked by moon's glow and cock's crow. But as the sun started peeking over the mountains, he realized that without some help, he would not be able to finish the doughnuts in time.

Up the stairs he went to his sons' bedroom. "Shawney, Irving," he said, "wake up!"

Shawney rubbed his eyes. "Papa, it isn't even daylight yet. Why do we need to get up?"

"I'm sorry, boys. I need your help in the bakery. The doughnuts are not finished. In a couple of hours, people will be lining up outside. Please! You must come and help me."

The boys yawned and grumbled as they stumbled sleepily down the stairs and into the bakery. Some of the grumbling was from Herbie, a friend of Irving's who was staying the night, and who was also very sleepy. But as soon as he was awake enough to realize what was happening, he said he would help, too.

The boys washed their hands. Papa pointed to a counter and said, "Thank you all for helping me. Please, come over to the sugaring trays and start putting sugar on the doughnuts."

Papa continued cutting and frying the doughnuts. Each time a batch of doughnuts came out of the fryer, he quickly passed them over to the boys. They put the doughnuts in one of the huge trays of sugar. Then they turned them over and sugared the other side.

The boys worked fast. Papa said to Herbie, "You are doing a fine job. Perhaps you could come and help from time to time. After tonight, it will be for pay."

Herbie smiled. He was glad he was doing such a good job helping his friend's papa.

After a while, Irving said, "We're almost out of sugar, Papa."

Papa couldn't stop cutting and frying. He waved his hand toward a huge can on a shelf above the counter. Since Herbie was very strong, he volunteered to get it down. With a groan, he took down the can and refilled the sugaring trays from it. When he was done, he set it back on the shelf.

The boys worked hard and steadily. To make the time pass quicker, they started reading some of the signs that Little Shawney's papa had hung in the bakery. Shawney read them his favorite sign.

> AS YOU GO THROUGH LIFE, MY BROTHER
> NO MATTER WHAT YOUR GOAL
> KEEP YOUR EYE UPON THE DOUGHNUT
> AND NOT UPON THE HOLE

Shawney loved this sign, because those were the first words that Papa had taught him to read when he was small.

Herbie said, "That sounds sort of silly—keep your eye upon the doughnut and not upon the hole. Why can't you look at the hole?"

Shawney did not think that it was silly at all, because Papa had explained it to him several times.

Shawney said, "Herbie, it means to look for the good things—not the things that aren't so good (like the hole)."

"Oh," said Herbie. "That's great!"

The boys kept working, hard. After awhile, Shawney's stomach started growling.

He looked at his father. "I'm getting hungry, Papa."

"I am sorry," said Papa. "But we cannot stop working, or we will not be ready in time." He looked at the clock. "It is six in the morning, and the bakery opens at seven. We have only one hour to get everything ready. Just eat a couple of doughnuts for now; you can have breakfast later."

Shawney's eyes grew wide with anticipation. He loved his papa's doughnuts, just like everyone else in town.

He picked up a doughnut and took a big bite. Then, he yelled and spit it out.

"Papa," he cried. "It tastes awful. There must be salt on it, instead of sugar!"

"No," said Papa. "It cannot be!"

Papa came over and picked up a doughnut. He took a bite and made a terrible face. What Shawney had said was true!

Papa turned to Herbie with a puzzled look. "Please, show me which can you emptied the sugar from."

Herbie pointed to a huge can on the shelf above.

"I am sorry, Herbie," said Papa. "But you grabbed the salt can by mistake."

He saw Herbie's anguished look. "No, Herbie. It is my fault. The salt can was right next to the sugar can. I was in a hurry and did not make it clear to you which one to get."

Papa was in despair. "It is almost time to open, and we do not have any doughnuts that we can sell. We will disappoint the whole town." He frowned. "And besides that, we will lose all of the money that I spent on the flour, eggs, sugar, and oil for these doughnuts."

"Papa," said Little Shawney, "isn't there some way we can get the salt off the doughnuts?"

Papa thought for a moment. His face broke into a smile. "There is one thing that we can try," he said. "I will put the doughnuts back into the oil. Hopefully, the hot oil will dissolve most of the salt that is on them."

He paused. "After that, you must throw out the salt. Then wash the trays, put sugar in them, and sugar the doughnuts very heavily. That will make up for any salt that might still be clinging to them. I will help you."

Papa and the boys worked frantically. From time to time, Shawney looked up from his work. It seemed that the hands of the big clock were going faster and faster. Would they finish before the bakery had to open?

At five minutes to seven, the doughnuts were done. The boys let out a WHOOP of celebration. They congratulated each other with sugary handshakes.

Shawney looked out. People were already lined up outside the store. He held his breath as customers came in and ordered huge sacks of doughnuts. He knew that people usually sampled a doughnut on their way out. He heard loud comments coming from some of the customers.

"OHHH! EXTRA SWEET!" said one. She turned to Shawney's papa. "A new recipe, Baker?"

"Why, yes," he said. "A NEW RECIPE. I'M SO GLAD YOU LIKE IT!"

"What do you call this new type of doughnut?"

Papa thought for a moment. He smiled. "I will call them 'SHAWNEY'S SUGAR CAKES.' He was the one who suggested the most important baking step, which makes them so good!"

The boys just winked at each other and grinned. It would be a sweet day, after all!

(My husband was the Little Shawney in this true story. He has fond memories of working in the bakery and helping his father. I am sure that is where he developed his love for bakery goods of all kinds.)

MEMORIES

Memories of Fast Nact;
Smiling stomachs,
Sugar-sweet dreams.
My baker father
Mixing, cutting, frying
By moon's glow and cock's crow.
But the night was too short,
Morning, too soon,
Sweet treats not ready, call in the platoon!
Troops into action,
Sons called to the sugary trenches,
All hands, white and sweet.
The battle
Soon in disarray
Salt in the sugaring tray.
A new plan!
Into the boiling oil,
The old coat removed.
Damaged spheres
Ready for a sprinkling
Of new sweetness.
Sugary sweet, delicate treat
Eager for savoring mouths to eat.
Secret recipe, don't repeat!

Orange Cake Doughnuts
(Makes about 2-1/2 dozen)

2 tablespoons vegetable oil
1 cup sugar
3 egg yolks
1 cup milk
Zest (rind) of one orange, grated

1 teaspoon orange extract
3 cups flour
1 tablespoon baking powder
3/4 teaspoon salt

Mix the oil, sugar, egg yolks, milk, orange zest, and orange extract. Blend well. Stir together flour, baking powder, and salt, and add to mixture. This will make a stiff dough. Chill one hour. Roll out on a lightly floured surface to 1/2-inch thickness. With a doughnut cutter, cut out rings. Reserve centers (holes) to fry separately. Heat 3 to 4 inches of oil in a heavy pan to 375 degrees F. Gently lower a few doughnut rings at a time into oil. Fry until golden brown and turn over. Let second side brown and then lift out with slotted spoon. Drain on paper towels. Dip in orange glaze (recipe below).

Orange Glaze

1 cup powdered sugar
1/2 cup orange juice

Stir powdered sugar and orange juice together to form glaze.

Buttermilk Drop Doughnuts
(Makes about 3-1/2 dozen)

2 cups flour
1/4 cup sugar
1/2 teaspoon salt
1 teaspoon baking powder
1/2 teaspoon baking soda
1/2 teaspoon ground nutmeg

1/4 cup vegetable oil
3/4 cup buttermilk (or plain milk plus
    2 tablespoons vinegar)
1 egg
Sugar and cinnamon

Heat oil (3 to 4 inches) in a heavy pan to 375 degrees F. Mix together flour, sugar, salt, baking powder, baking soda, and nutmeg. Add oil, buttermilk, and egg. Beat with fork until smooth. Drop batter by teaspoonful (do not make too large, or they will not cook through) into hot oil. Fry about 3 minutes, or until golden brown on both sides. Drain on paper towels. Immediately roll in sugar and cinnamon.

Dancing Goats

by Linda Batlin

I remember my first time away from home. I was ten years old. I spent that summer of 1957 at Camp Waziyatah on Lake McWain in Maine. The boys' camp was on one side of the lake. On the other was the girls' camp, where I spent two months, and where I learned so many things.

Before going to camp, I had to have labels with my name on all my sheets, towels and clothes, including my panties. I sat with my mom as she showed me different stitches for sewing on my "Linda Batlin Camp Waziyatah" labels. We spent several afternoons after school in the spring, sewing together at the dining room table. That's how I learned to sew.

One day I asked, "Mom, what will I do at camp?"

"Oh," she said, "there will be all kinds of things, like swimming and horses. And there will be girls your age, so you can make new friends."

This really intrigued me, because out in the country where we lived, there really wasn't anyone else my age, and I didn't have many friends.

After what seemed like years, the end of June finally came. We drove from Maryland, where I lived, to Maine. I was so excited! What would it be like to be away from home? From my family? So many questions and things to wonder about! But eventually, I realized that it would be a great. There would be so many new things to learn!

Mom and Dad dropped me off at camp. Then, they went on a long car trip to Canada. They timed their trip so they could be back for Parent's Weekend before returning home.

Everything at camp was structured. The campers were divided by age groups, from the 8-year-olds to the 17-year-olds. We slept in cabins. I stayed in a rustic one with seven other girls my age. The cabins were very simple, with eight beds, shelves for clothes, and a bathroom.

There was a big dining room where we ate all our meals. Each cabin had its assigned table, and food was served family style. If anyone was late to a meal, or misbehaved, they had to sweep the docks by the lake — something I had to do a couple of times. Sometimes, we had cookouts by the lake. We cooked hot dogs on the campfire and had great fun. We even made wonderfully gooey s'mores, with marshmallows, chocolate bars and graham crackers.

During the day, we were always busy. There were so many activities — like horseback riding, canoeing, archery, arts and crafts, and dance. And swimming. I didn't know how to swim. I had never been in a body of water bigger than a bathtub. So going into Lake McWain was a little scary. It took awhile, but I learned to float on my back by myself, without anyone supporting me. And I learned some swim strokes, too. There was a wood dock that separated the shallow water from the deep water. Even though I only stayed in the shallow part, I was so proud of myself. For the first time in my life, I felt independent. I could make my own decisions! If I got dirty, no one told me to go wash, so sometimes I didn't and just stayed dirty.

And I did make friends. Especially with Marjorie, who came from Pennsylvania and lived in my cabin. In fact, she was my first "best friend." We both loved animals, and we spent lots of time with each other. Sometimes, we explored together.

On one of our explorations, we found a place that had some cages with rabbits in them. We went to Mr. Turner, who was in charge of the animals at camp.

"Mr. Turner," I said, "The rabbits are really cute. Could we help you take care of them?"

"I guess so," he replied, ". . . if you REALLY want to."

"Oh, yes," we shouted at the same time. "We REALLY, REALLY want to!"

He showed us how to give the rabbits their food and water, and how to hold them so they wouldn't kick us with their furry hind feet. Marjorie and I fed them every day. We loved holding and petting them.

One day, Mr. Turner came in while we were feeding the rabbits. He said "You two are doing a great job. I guess you're real 'rabbit girls'!"

We were delighted. From then on, we called ourselves the "rabbit girls."

One day, I realized that Parents' Weekend was coming. The parents would watch as the kids demonstrated the activities they were doing and the things they were learning.

Mom and Dad came back from their Canadian trip. To show how independent I had become, I didn't bother to get cleaned up, or to comb my hair. Mom was definitely not impressed (at least, not the right way). She took one look at me and frowned.

"You're dirty!" she said. "Don't you ever wash?"

"No one said that I had to," I retorted. "So, I decided that I don't need to wash every day."

This didn't go over well with Mom. I had to promise to wash if I wanted to stay at camp the rest of the summer. I begrudgingly agreed.

The next part of my demonstration went better. I showed Mom and Dad how I had learned to float. They were very pleased.

For lunch that day we had a simple hamburger stew with onions and green peppers. Mom liked it so much that she started making it at home and called it "hunter stew."

Camp Waziyatah had a series of events. The following weekend was Boys' Weekend, when the boys from the other side of the lake came to visit for a Saturday afternoon. The older girls got all gooey and silly over this. Marjorie and I weren't the least bit interested in seeing the boys. We got ourselves excused from participating in the games and picnic. Instead, we went to visit the rabbits, which lived away from the main part of camp. As we cared for the rabbits, we talked about what we would do for the variety show that the younger girls were putting on for the older girls. The show was in three weeks.

Mr. Turner was there. "We have a couple of goats here," he said. "Maybe you could teach them to dance and do a routine on stage."

"Dance?" we said, looking doubtful.

He told us that he done this before and that he would be happy to coach us and the goats in the fine points of dance. We agreed, so he introduced us to the two goats. I got to work with Gertrude, who had a dark brown coat. Marjorie got Samantha, whose coat was light tan.

Dance lessons were held every afternoon outside the crafts building, after we finished taking care of the rabbits. If it rained, we went inside. It was easy. The routine was always the same. Marjorie and I put one foot behind the other, looked at our respective goats, and held up two fingers, with a "goat cookie" or treat between them. Gertrude and Samantha stood on their hind legs, after carefully studying our fingers for a moment. Then they ate their treats and put their front hooves on our shoulders.

At this point, Mr. Turner put a Strauss waltz on the record player. I looked at Gertrude at eye level and put my hands on her shoulders. Then, with her front hooves on mine, we danced. Marjorie did the same with Samantha. It was awkward at first, because none of us had ever danced before. But eventually, all four of us learned to waltz (sort of) in time to the music. Marjorie and I were so pleased with Gertrude and Samantha's love of music and dancing that we looked forward to our rehearsals.

At last, the night of the variety show came. It was a warm, clear evening, and all the stars were out. Marjorie and I had given the goats a bath that afternoon so they would look (and smell) good for their performance. We put on clean shorts and blouses and socks so we would look good. We were a little nervous, but we figured that was okay.

The show was in the camp auditorium. We stood outside, waiting our turn to go on stage. There was a clown routine before us.

"Let's rehearse while we're waiting," I said.

"Yes," said Marjorie. "We don't want Gertrude and Samantha to be nervous."

So we practiced with several goat cookies. Each time we held one up, Gertrude and Samantha got up on their hind legs, gazed hungrily at our hands, balanced their front hooves on our shoulders, and ate their treat. We could hear the audience cheering the other performers. Soon, they would be cheering us!

Finally, it was our turn. We led Gertrude and Samantha on stage by their collars. The auditorium was packed! Marjorie and I each took a goat cookie out of our pocket, held it up, and put one foot back. Mr. Turner started the music. Gertrude looked at the audience, then at me, then at the audience, and walked away. Samantha did the same. The audience started laughing!

We led Gertrude and Samantha back to center stage. We held the cookies up again. The goats just stood there and looked at us. The clown from the previous act came out and pranced behind us as we tried to get the goats to stand up and take their dance positions. That made everyone laugh harder.

After a couple of minutes, we and the goats were escorted off the stage by the emcee. Gertrude and Samantha didn't seem to mind, but Marjorie and I were devastated.

Mr. Turner came up to us. "I don't know why they wouldn't dance like in our rehearsals," said Marjorie. "They must have had stage fright!"

"Hmm," said Mr. Turner. "You didn't happen to rehearse with treats just before you came on, did you?"

Suddenly, it hit me. Gertrude and Samantha didn't have stage fright. They just weren't hungry anymore. I realized that Gertrude's and Samantha's love of music and dance was really just a great love of food!

49

After that, Marjorie and I didn't try to make the goats dance again. But we continued to care for the rabbits. We promised to write to each other after camp ended. We never saw each other again, but we did write for years, until we each went to college and started new lives. We always signed our letters "From one rabbit girl to another."

That trip to camp at age ten was my first time away from home. I learned so many things that summer that have stayed with me through life. I learned to sew, and I learned to float in water. I was introduced to hunter stew. Later on, I learned to make it, and cooked it for my college roommates. I learned to care for rabbits. And I learned that goats will only dance if they feel like it. I got my first taste of independence that summer. But most importantly, I learned what it was like to have a best friend, and that was the best lesson of all.

Hunter Stew

1 large onion
2 green peppers
1 to 2 pounds ground beef (I now use buffalo)
1 clove garlic
Pinch of basil
Salt and pepper to taste

Chop up onion and peppers. Sauté in a frying pan and remove to a bowl. In the same pan, sauté ground meat until brown, and add seasonings. Pour off excess fat. Return vegetables to pan and mix for a minute to combine flavors. Serve over cooked noodles or rice, with a green salad on the side.

S'mores

1 chocolate bar
2 graham crackers
Marshmallows

Break chocolate bar into squares. Put 4 squares on a graham cracker. Roast 2 or 3 marshmallows until they are runny inside. Place on the chocolate. Put on 4 more chocolate squares. Top with the second graham cracker, and press down. Enjoy! (Be sure to have a paper towel handy in case your s'more drips.)

One Tough Bird

by Joyce Nelson

"You're running around like a chicken with its head cut off." That was my dad's favorite saying. Actually, we were like headless chicks, flying around in circles, bouncing into each other on purpose. Because of a big summer storm, we had been shut up in our hot house all morning, like cooped-up chickens. We wished we could be playing outside—and I'm sure our parents agreed.

After what seemed like hours, we got the "all clear" from Mom.

"All right, you kids, go play outside."

My sister Kathy, who was nine, my brother David, who was seven, and I (who was eight) raced through the open screen door, bolted off the porch, and started running around. We looked just like—well, like chickens with their heads cut off.

We knew all about chickens, because we raised them. They provided eggs for breakfast and meat for supper. They had their own house, called a "coop," and their own fenced yard. They ate just about anything, from berries and bugs to their favorite, Purina Chicken Chow.

Sometimes, I fed the chickens. We had black ones, white ones, black-and-white ones, and a dark red one. Using a blue coffee can, I scooped chicken feed from a bag and flung it on the ground, calling the chickens like my folks and my grandmother did: "Here chick, chick, chick, here chick, chick, chick."

Most of the chickens were easygoing, and we liked them. But not Rooster, the dark red one. He was funny looking. He had long black tail feathers that stuck up and glistened in the sun. We always laughed at his "crown" (which was really called a "comb"). It was a piece of red skin that was scalloped on the edges and stood straight up, like a Mohawk haircut. He also had a "wattle," a red piece of skin that hung down under his chin. And he had long red earlobes that drooped on either side of his head. But he wasn't just funny looking. He was also mean, like an—well, like an old rooster. All of us kids hated Rooster. I was always scared of him.

One day when I was four, Rooster had run after me, chasing and pecking my bare legs.

"Daddy, help me," I screamed. "Make him stop!" I ran as quickly as I could, but Rooster was FAST. Daddy scooped me up in his strong arms.

"There, there," he said, "you're safe with Daddy." I clung to him as he patted my back, but I also saw that he was trying not to laugh. He knew that crazy cock-a-doodle-do would never try to bother him. Rooster knew Daddy was at the top of the pecking order. He knew daddy was BOSS.

But Rooster still bullied everyone else, including Mom. Whenever we gathered eggs, Kathy and I teamed up. We took turns being the lookout. When I was lookout, I went to a spot just outside the fence and threw chicken feed into the yard. When Rooster came to peck at it, Kathy sneaked inside the coop and snatched the eggs.

But one day, our plan went awry. We were getting ready to join our cousins for a picnic in Forest Park. Mom sent us to the coop to get eggs for the potato salad.

It was my turn to gather the eggs. Kathy stationed herself in the lookout spot and threw chicken feed over the fence. Quietly, I tiptoed to the coop, went in, and grabbed the eggs. I stuck my head out and looked both ways to see if Rooster was around, just like you do when you're crossing a street. The coast was clear. I strolled confidently out of the coop.

Suddenly, Rooster appeared out of nowhere and attacked my legs.

"Get away!" I yelled as I raced away. I ran through the gate and closed it. I knew I was safe. Unfortunately, things hadn't gone as well for the eggs. In my hurry, I had dropped the egg basket. Every single one of the eggs was broken. Now, it wasn't Rooster I was afraid of—it was my mom. What would she say?

Rooster must have realized he had won. He crowed, just like he was laughing at me. I was madder than a—well, madder than a wet hen. I promised myself that one day, I would get even with him.

I ran to the house and burst into the kitchen. "Mom," I sobbed, "I'm sorry, but Rooster chased me again and I dropped the eggs." I put on my saddest face. "Can't you make him stop?" I pleaded.

Mom saw the egg and eggshells on my sad little face. She smiled. "Don't worry about the eggs," she said. "I'm glad you're safe." As she wiped my face, she said, "Rooster is a tough old bird. I'll see what I can do."

Soon, it was time to go. Mom got out the special box where she kept the things we only used for picnics—a red-and-white checkered tablecloth, blue and yellow plastic plates, and plastic forks and spoons. Dad always said "Money doesn't grow on trees, you know," so we washed and dried the plastic utensils after every picnic and put them back in the picnic box. There was plenty of space in the box for the foods we were bringing that day—potato salad, bananas, windmill cookies, lemonade, and some watermelon.

We were also bringing fried chicken, my all-time favorite. But we didn't have it yet, because Granny, who lived with us, still had to catch and fry some. She grabbed the "chicken catcher" and went into the chicken yard. It was a long wire, about as thick as a clothes hanger, with a hooked end. She snagged a chicken and pulled it toward her. Then she grabbed it by the head so she wouldn't get pecked.

Granny quickly rotated her hand and wrist, wringing off the head. The chicken landed on its feet and ran around in circles like a—well, like a chicken with its head cut off. Then she caught a second one. Kathy, David, and I stood fascinated, staring at the headless chickens running around.

Next, Granny cleaned the chickens. She used hot water to soften the feathers. Then she plucked them. As always, there were a few little pin feathers left. She rolled up a newspaper, lit it, and waved the fire over those little pin feathers to burn them off. We held our noses. The singed feathers stank to high heaven.

Granny handed the now-naked chickens to David and told him to take them to Mom. Kathy and I followed him into the house. Mom put the chickens in the sink and washed them. We always laughed that she was giving the chickens a bath. Then, she dried the chickens and put them on a cutting board. With a sharp knife, she sliced each chicken open, right down the middle. Then she pulled out the guts.

David said "Neat-o," but Kathy and I made faces. Mom threw away the guts, but she saved the gizzards and livers for cooking.

I think Mom knew she had to get Kathy's mind, and mine, on other things. She asked, "Do you want to hear a chicken story?"

"Yes!" we said. We grabbed chairs and sat down. We knew this would be good.

"When your father and I were newlyweds, he brought home a live chicken and asked me to fix it for supper. He took it down to the basement and put it in a washtub for the night."

She sighed. "I didn't have a clue about how to cook a live chicken. I wanted to please your father and make him happy. But I had never taken the life of any animal."

She told us how she started cleaning the house to get her mind off the chicken. But the problem still lurked in the back of her mind all day. Finally, she couldn't put it off any longer—soon, Dad would be home from work, and would be hungry. So she trudged to the basement to transform that chicken into dinner. Somehow, she had to cut its head off.

"I picked up a hatchet and grabbed the chicken's neck. When I was about to whack it, the chicken looked up at me and squawked 'baaaawwwk'! I just couldn't do it! I knew I couldn't chop its head off. I tried again. And again. But that 'baaaawwwk' stopped my swinging arm every time!"

"What did you do?" we asked.

"Well," she said, "After trying for an hour, I dropped the hatchet, ran up the stairs, and cooked. Your father was expecting fried chicken, but what he got for supper was turnips and cabbage."

Yuck! I didn't like turnips or cabbage, so I was glad that Mom had finally learned how to kill and fix a chicken!

We watched as she cut the chicken for our picnic into just the right sized pieces. She rolled the parts in seasoned flour, then cooked them in hot grease. When it was done, we helped her pack the fried chicken in the picnic box.

Now that everything was packed, my sister, brother, and I ran to the car. "Dibs on a window seat," yelled Kathy. "Dibs on the other window seat," I yelled.

That left David sitting in the middle.

"It's my turn for a window seat," he whined.

He knew that he had been had. It was hot, so the best place in the car was next to a rolled-down window. Air conditioning for cars had not yet been invented.

We thought that if we were already sitting in the car, we would get to the picnic sooner. Wrong! We bickered more about who got a window seat, pushed each other out of the car, and ran around. Dad came out of the house, carrying the picnic box. "Get into the car!" he yelled. "You're running around like. . ." Well, you know the rest!

The drive to Forest Park seemed to take forever. As usual, we kept asking, "Are we there yet?" And as usual, Dad answered, "Not yet."

To keep us quiet, Dad told a story. It was about a pet chicken that he had when he was seven. Growing up on a small farm, he made friends with all the animals. But one animal was special—Petey, the chicken.

"We were best friends," said Dad. "Petey followed me everywhere, just like a puppy. Sometimes, I tucked him under my arm and carried him like a football. When I petted him, I was careful not to ruffle his feathers. We trusted each other."

One day, Dad came home from school, but he couldn't find Petey. He looked everywhere—inside the coop and in the back yard.

"Petey, Petey" he called. But Petey didn't come running like he usually did.

Dad hurried into the kitchen. "Have you seen Petey?" he asked his mom. She got a sad look on her face, like the time when she told him his pet turtle had died.

"Sonny," she said (that was Dad's nickname), "remember how when Petey was little, I told you that when he became skillet sized, we would eat him for supper?"

Dad looked at her in shock.

"Now, you know that's the way of the farm," she said. "We raise animals for food."

Dad glanced at the big black iron skillet on the stove. Inside the pan was a chicken, frying in hot grease.

"Not Petey!" he cried. He got a sick feeling in his stomach, and tears welled up in his eyes. He bolted from the kitchen and raced out to the chicken coop. He wanted Petey back.

At suppertime, Dad's family gathered around the table. In the middle was a platter of fried chicken. Dad sat in his chair but didn't eat a bite. When he looked at the chicken, he imagined his brown feathered friend, looking at him with sad eyes. It was several years before Dad understood that Petey made the ultimate sacrifice, giving his life so that Dad's family could eat.

"But that night," Dad said, "I went to bed hungry because I couldn't eat Petey."

When I heard that story, I felt sad for Dad and Petey. But not for long, because we were finally at the park.

We darted out of the car, whooping and hollering after spotting our cousins Joy, who was six, and Walter, who was three. We all tumbled and rolled down the hills in the park until we were so dizzy we staggered.

Mom, Dad, Granny, and Aunt Edie found a perfect spot for the picnic. Then Dad hollered, "Come and eat. You're running around like a chicken with its head cut off."

We came and sat down. The food on the table was fit for a king . . . and those two chickens, fresh, fried to a golden brown, smelled so good.

We said grace. After the prayer, I dived in. One of the chickens was juicy and tender. I licked my fingers and smacked my lips as I ate. But the other one—the one that used to have dark red feathers—he was a tough old bird. But unlike my dad with Petey, it didn't bother me at all to chew on that chicken's leg. Mmmmmmm good. This was one rooster that wouldn't be chasing me any more!

Fried Chicken

1 frying chicken, cut up
1 cup flour
1 teaspoon salt
1/2 teaspoon pepper
Enough oil to cover the bottom of a large frying pan to about 1 inch deep

Wash the chicken and pat dry. Mix together the flour, salt, and pepper. Put the flour mixture onto a plate and roll each piece of chicken, coating it well. Pour the oil into a large heavy skillet and heat. When the oil is hot, carefully slide in the chicken pieces. Lower heat. Cook with a lid on for about 20 minutes or until the chicken pieces are golden brown on the bottom. Remove lid and turn pieces over. Cook another 15 minutes or so with the lid off (this will allow the chicken to crisp up). Turn chicken as needed. Be sure to fry the chicken until it is completely done, with no pink showing. Drain well on absorbent paper.

Rooster's Dumplings
(Chicken and Dumplings)

Broth

2 quarts water (8 cups)
3 chicken bouillon cubes
1 chicken, cut up (or 5 chicken thighs)

Put ingredients into a 4-quart pan. Simmer one hour, or until chicken is very tender. Remove chicken from broth and cool slightly. Pick chicken meat from bones. Discard bones. Save broth.

Dumplings

While the chicken is cooking, make dumplings:

3 cups flour
1-1/2 teaspoons salt
1-1/2 cups canned chicken broth

Combine ingredients and mix into a stiff dough. If needed, work in more flour. Roll dough thinly, like a pie crust (about 1/4 inch thick). Cut into strips, 1 inch wide by 3 inches long. Bring broth in which the chicken was cooked to a rapid boil. Drop dumplings into broth. Boil about 10 minutes. Leave the lid off the pot, so pot doesn't boil over. Add chicken to pot, reheat and serve. Mmmmmm good!

The Unexpected Passover Visitor

by Ed Winograd

Author's Note: The *Passover Seder* includes many more rituals, ceremonial objects, songs, and foods than the ones described here. I've omitted these to keep the story from being too long.

As Deborah Weinstein lay face down on her bed, she heard her mother call. "Time to come downstairs, kids. You know what tonight is!"

"Just a minute," she called back. "I have to finish something."

Something was her diary. She quickly scribbled a few more sentences:

> Paul's being a royal pain, like always. He thinks Rachel and I are pests because Mom and Dad ask him to drive us places. And Sam's always asking us questions. Believe me, we both know why "brother" and "bother" sound almost the same!

She took two keys out of her pocket. She used one to lock the diary. Then she got a box from her desk drawer and put the diary in it. She locked the box and put it back in the drawer. She put both keys in her pocket and went down to the dining room.

Her mother and father were already at the table. So was three-year-old Samuel. This was a very special night, thought Deborah. The night of the Seder, the ceremonial meal that Jews hold each year on Passover, to celebrate how God freed the ancient Israelites from slavery in Egypt.

Each year, her family took turns reading the Passover story aloud from the *Hagaddah*. She loved reading the story, and singing Passover songs. She also loved the "festive meal" that was part of the Seder, and the special foods that went with it.

As Deborah sat down, Rachel, who was nine, came in. She had watercolor paint on her hands. "Wow," said Deborah. "You *really* need the ritual handwashing that we'll do tonight!" Rachel stuck out her tongue. But before Deborah could say anything, their mother stopped her. "Rachel," she said, "Go wash your hands before the Seder starts."

As Rachel stomped off, the front door opened and shut with a bang. Sixteen-year-old Paul dashed in and sat down. He was wearing a baseball cap. And headphones for his MP3 player. His father pointed at his head. Paul sheepishly took off the cap and headphones.

Just then, Rachel came back. "Daddy," she yelled. "Paul's doing two things wrong. I was only doing one!" Her father sighed. "Kids," he said. "Your mom and I worked hard to make our Seder special. Can't we all be nice to each other tonight?"

If he expected a response, he didn't get one. "All right," he said. "It's time to start." Everyone picked up their Hagaddah and turned to the first page.

Deborah's mother turned to her. "Will you please light the candles?" she said. Rachel made a face. "Why does she get to light the candles? Why can't I?" Her mother looked at her. "I told you before," she said. "Deborah's twelve and will have her *Bat Mitzvah* in December. In honor of that, she gets to light the candles."

Rachel stuck her tongue out again. Her mother saw and eyeballed her. She stopped. Then Deborah lit the candles and recited the blessing:

Baruch atah Adonai, Eloheinu melech ha-olam, asher kidshanu b'mitzvotav, v'tsivanu l'hadlik ner shel Yom Tov.

She also recited a blessing that thanked God for keeping her family alive to celebrate Passover.

"Very good," said her mother. "Now we'll pour the first cup of wine." Deborah watched as her parents poured the first of their four small cups of wine for the Seder. Paul also had wine, which he could legally drink for religious purposes. But the younger kids had grape juice.

"Why can't I have wine?" said Deborah. "I've been studying hard for my Bat Mitzvah. I think I deserve some, too." Paul snickered. "You can't until your Bat Mitzvah," he said. "Until then, you're still a little girl."

Deborah started to reply, but her mother stopped her. "Please," she said. "Let's really make this night different from other nights. Like your dad said, let's try to get along well together!"

Deborah's family said the *kiddush* and drank the first cup of wine (or grape juice). Then they continued reading from the Hagaddah. Her father washed his hands on behalf of everyone at the Seder. They dipped their *karpas* in salt water (which represents the tears of the Jewish slaves in Egypt) and recited the ancient blessing.

Then came one of Deborah's favorite parts. On a tray was a pile of *matzoh*, covered by a cloth. Her father took a piece from the middle and broke it in half. He put the first half back, then went out of the room and hid the second half. This was the *afikomon*. Later, the kids would search for it; whoever found it would get a reward. This was the last time Deborah would do that. After her Bat Mitzvah, she would be considered an adult in the Jewish community, rather than a child.

Her father came back. He uncovered the matzoh and held up the tray. Then he read from the Hagaddah. "This is the bread of affliction, which our ancestors ate in the land of Egypt." He paused, then read again. "Let all who are hungry come and eat."

Just then, there was a knock at the door. Everyone looked surprised. Who could it possibly be?

Deborah's mother went to the door and opened it. An old man was there. He looked like he hadn't eaten for days. His face and hands were dirty, and he was wearing a dirty robe. His long hair was mostly white, with patches of gray. He had a long beard. His sandals were old and looked like they might fall apart at any time.

He smiled at Deborah's mother. "I was wandering outside, when I heard your invitation."

"What invitation?" she stammered.

"Your very kind invitation," he said. "Let all who are hungry come and eat."

By now, everyone had come to the door. What would her parents do, Deborah wondered. And how had he heard the invitation? The front door and windows were all closed.

Deborah's father looked at her mother. She nodded. "Come in," he said. "Please, come share our Seder."

"Thank you," said the visitor. "But I would like to wash first." Deborah's mother pointed up the stairs. "Please go ahead," she said. "The bathroom is to the left." The visitor thanked her and went up.

Deborah's family went back to the dining room. Her father brought another chair. Her mother brought a place setting and a Hagaddah. Everyone sat down. Soon, the visitor came back. His hands and face were clean.

"You look hungry," said Deborah's mother. "We won't eat for awhile. But I'll bring you something now." The visitor shook his head. "No, please don't interrupt the Seder for me."

Deborah's father covered the matzoh. After awhile, everyone poured the second cup of wine or juice. It was time now for one of Deborah's favorite parts, the reading of the Four Questions. By tradition, the Four Questions are read, in Hebrew and English, by the youngest person who can do so. In Deborah's family, that was Rachel.

She read the first question, in English:

"Why is this night different from all other nights?"

and then in Hebrew:

Mah nishtanah haloolah hazeh mikol halaylot?

As Rachel began the second question, Paul leaned over and whispered in her ear. "It's not *haloolah*, dummy. It's *halailah*." Rachel pouted. "Mom," she yelled, "Paul's being mean!"

Before anyone could say anything, the visitor turned to Paul. "Is that really what you think of your sister?" he said. "What are you talking about?" Paul asked. "The word you whispered," said the visitor. "The one that starts with *d*. And ends with *y*."

Paul was dumbstruck. He had whispered into Rachel's ear. How had the visitor heard it? "No, I guess not," he stammered. "It's just that—"

"Whether she read perfectly or not, she tried her best. That is acceptable in the eyes of God, I can assure you."

The visitor turned to Rachel. "Go on, my dear. I'm sure you'll do fine." Sure enough, she did an excellent job on all of the remaining questions.

After the Four Questions, everyone took turns reading the answers from the Hagaddah. Deborah loved how the answers showed what a special night the Seder was. And soon came another of her favorite parts, the tale of the "Four Children." It speaks of four types of children to whom the story of the Israelites' escape from Egypt must be told: the wise child, the wicked child, the simple child, and child who is too young to ask about it. Deborah had always felt that each of the four types represented someone in her family.

When her mother read about the wise child, Deborah thought "That's easy. It's me!" When the visitor read about the wicked child, she thought "That's Paul. He's always trying to put me down. Sometimes he's a royal pain!"

Deborah heard her mother gasp. She looked around. Everyone was staring at her.

"What's wrong?" she asked. Rachel piped up. "You said Paul was the wicked child!" Deborah was shocked. She knew she had only thought that. How had the others heard it?

"Deborah," said her mother. "I think you owe Paul an—"

The visitor raised his hand to stop her. He looked at Deborah. "Don't worry," he said. "Everyone has unkind thoughts sometimes about other people. Even about their siblings." He looked Deborah straight in the eye. "So," he said. "Do you really think your brother is wicked? Or just that he's a 'royal pain'?"

"Sometimes when I'm really mad, I think he's a pain," she admitted. She looked at Paul. "But I don't really think you're either of those things." She paused. "I didn't think I said it out loud. But if I did, I apologize."

Her father smiled at her, then at the visitor. "I've been trying to get the kids to learn to apologize to each other for a long time," he said. "Thank you." The visitor smiled. "Please," he said, "let us get back to the Hagaddah."

Deborah read the next passage, about the "simple child," who is "easily confused."

"That's Rachel," said Paul's voice. "I always have to tell her things twice. She's such a little pest."

Now, everyone was staring at Paul. "What?" he said.

"You called Rachel a pest," said Deborah. "Just like you call me." Paul was amazed. "No, I didn't!" he said. "But I *was* thinking it," he added embarrassedly.

The visitor turned to Paul. "Don't be hard on yourself," he said. "There's no harm in thinking that sometimes." He smiled. "It's all right, because I can feel that deep in your heart, you love her."

Paul turned to Rachel. "I'm sorry if I called you that." He said *if* in a strange way, like he wasn't sure he had really done it. His father started to say something, but he saw that the visitor was pointing at the Hagaddah. "Okay," he said. "It's Paul's turn now."

Paul read the passage about the last child, the youngest one, who "hardly knew how to ask a question." When he stopped, everyone heard Rachel's voice.

"That's Sam, 'cause he's the youngest. But he knows how to ask questions. He's always bugging me, asking me 'why this' and 'why that.' What a bother!"

The room went silent. All except Sam, who started to cry. His mother picked him up and comforted him. "Rachel," she said. "The Seder is hardly the place to say that Sam is a bother!"

"I didn't say anything!" said Rachel. The visitor smiled at her. "But did you think it?"

"I guess so. But—"

"Sam is very young. I'm sure he asks many questions. So, have you ever told him that he's a bother?"

"Maybe a couple of times."

"You must remember," said the visitor, "that words can wound. You don't have to hit or push someone to hurt them."

Rachel got up. She walked to her mother, who was still holding Sam. She wiped the tears off his face and whispered something. He giggled. She went back to her chair and sat down. Her mother turned to the visitor to say "Thank you." But he just pointed at the Hagaddah. So the family went back to their ceremony again.

After everyone drank the second cup of wine or juice, they all performed the ritual handwashing that Deborah had teased Rachel about. Then came another of Deborah's favorite parts, the "festive meal." This year, her mother had outdone herself. There was beef brisket, matzoh ball soup, apple *kugel* and green beans. For dessert, she had made *macaroons*.

After the meal, Deborah, Rachel, and Sam went through the house and searched for the afikomon. Sam found it and got a small toy as a reward. Deborah realized this was the last time for her. She felt sad, but she was also glad to know that after her Bat Mitzvah, she would be considered an adult in the Jewish religion.

When the kids returned, Deborah's father broke the afikomon and gave a piece to everyone to eat. Deborah knew this was important, because the Seder cannot end until this is done. She also knew that no one could eat anything after this. But she didn't want to, after the wonderful Seder meal.

After everyone drank the third cup of wine or juice, the visitor asked if he could use the rest room. "Of course," said Deborah's mother. "But please don't take long. The next thing in the Hagaddah is Elijah's cup. We'll wait for you." He turned as he headed up the stairs. "Please, don't stop on account of me. I insist."

Deborah knew that the ritual of Elijah's cup was very important. According to Jewish tradition, the prophet Elijah never died. He was carried to heaven in a fiery chariot. Since then, he is said to visit every Seder. At each one, a glass of wine is poured into a special cup, which is reserved for Elijah. Then, someone opens the door to let him enter. Deborah's family poured the fourth cup of wine or juice. Her father poured wine into "Elijah's cup." Then he got up and opened the front door. He came back and held up the cup, as the family sang a song for Elijah.

Eliyahu ha-navi, Eliyahu ha-tishvi,
Eliyahu, Eliyahu, Eliyahu ha-giladi

When they were done, he set the cup down. "That's strange," he said. "The cup is empty." Deborah looked surprised. "That's impossible," she said. "I've been watching it the whole time. I know the words to the song, so I didn't have to look at the Hagaddah."

"That reminds me," said her mother. "Please see if our visitor is all right. He should be here. He's as much a part of our Seder as we are." Deborah went upstairs. There was no one in the bathroom. She looked in all the bedrooms. Still no sign of him. She came back to the dining room.

"Did you ask him to come down?" said her mother. "I couldn't," said Deborah. "He wasn't there." She paused. "Did he come down and leave?" Everyone shook their head.

The visitor had said not to wait, so they went on. After a while, they sang Passover songs that Deborah loved, like *Adir Hu*, *Echod Mi Yodea*, and *Chad Gadya*. Shortly after that, they reached the end of the service. Everyone drank their final cup of wine or juice. They recited the final prayer. They had kept the commandment to tell and celebrate the story of the exodus from Egypt in their Seder, as Jews everywhere have done for thousands of years.

When the Seder was over, everyone helped clean up. They were all thinking about the mysterious visitor.

"Such a nice man," said Deborah's mother. "And we never even found out his name." Her father nodded. "I'd like to," he said. "He helped make peace among the kids. I want to thank him for that."

As they talked, the kids all insisted they hadn't said out loud the things that the visitor talked to them about. "I don't know," said their mother. "Sometimes we all blurt things out without thinking. There's nothing unusual about that."

When everything was cleaned up, Deborah went to her room. She opened her desk drawer and took out the box. She took the keys out of her pocket and opened the box and the diary. Then she put the keys back in her pocket. She picked up a pen and started writing in her diary. Then she stopped and looked at the top of the page. Her eyes went wide. She dashed down the stairs, into the kitchen. Her parents were still there.

"Mom, Dad," said Deborah. "You know the things we all thought we didn't say, but the visitor talked to us about? Like that Paul was a pain, or Rachel was a pest, or Sam was a bother?"

"Yes," said her mother. "Please, don't remind me."

"I had forgotten. All those things were in my diary. In what I wrote just before the Seder." She paused. "When he went upstairs, he must have opened it and read about them."

Her mother looked puzzled. "Don't you kept your diary in a locked box? And doesn't it have a lock?" Deborah nodded. "Yes," she said. "And I had the keys in my pocket. Look." She took out the keys and showed them to her parents.

That was very strange, she thought. Then it hit her. "There's some other strange things, too. Remember how he heard Dad say 'Let all who are hungry come and eat.' How could he? The front door and windows were closed. And how he heard what Paul said, even though he whispered it in Rachel's ear?"

She paused. "And what about how we kids said things out loud that we didn't think we did? All of them were from my diary. He must have somehow read them, then made us say them out loud."

Her mother and father both looked doubtful.

"And what about Elijah's cup?" said Deborah. "Why was it empty, when I had watched it the whole time? And what about how he disappeared, right when we reached the part about Elijah?"

"What are you telling us?" said her father. "You're not saying that he was really—"

"Why not?" said Deborah.

"This is the twenty-first century," he said. "Miracles don't happen any more."

"Oh yeah? What about how he got us kids to stop fighting with each other. What do you call that?"

"You've got me there," said her father.

"Well," said her mother, "we'll certainly have a new story to tell at next year's Seder. And in the future. I guess we can thank our unexpected Passover visitor for that!"

Glossary:

Note: In the story, the *first* occurrence of each of the following words and phrases is in italics.

Adir Hu	"Mighty Is He."
Afikomon	Half of the middle piece of matzoh. After it is hidden, the children look for it. Whoever finds it gets a small reward.
Bat/Bar Mitzvah	The coming-of-age ceremony at which a Jewish girl (Bat Mitzvah) or boy (Bar Mitzvah) becomes an adult in the Jewish community.
Chad Gadya	A song in which each verse builds on earlier ones, like "The House that Jack Built."
Echod Mi Yodea	"Who Knows One?" A song about important Jewish beliefs and history.
Hagaddah	A book that includes the Seder ritual and tells the story of the ancient Jews' exodus from slavery in Egypt.
Karpas	A vegetable set out on a ceremonial plate. Most families use parsley for it.
Kiddush	The prayer said before drinking wine.
Kugel	A baked pudding, usually served as a side dish.
Macaroon	A small cookie, usually made from ground nuts.
Matzoh	A flat, cracker-like unleavened bread. When the Israelites escaped from Egypt, they had no time to let their bread rise. Matzoh is a reminder of this.
Passover	The holiday which celebrates the Jews' escape from slavery in Egypt.
Seder	The ceremonial meal held during Passover, at which the Hagaddah is read.

Matzoh Balls

1 tablespoon potato starch
1/4 cup matzoh meal
1/3 cup water
Pinch of salt
Vegetable broth to taste
Water for boiling with vegetable broth

1. Mix starch, matzoh meal, water, and salt, and refrigerate for 30 minutes.
2. While mixture is cooling, add vegetable broth to water, and boil.
3. Roll mixture into balls (about eight) and drop into boiling water.
4. Lower heat and boil for 20 minutes.
5. Remove matzoh balls with a slotted spoon.
6. Place on a cookie sheet that has been lightly sprayed with a non-stick coating. Bake at 350 degrees for 10 minutes.
7. Serve with vegetable broth, 3-4 matzoh balls per serving.

Note: If desired, make matzoh balls ahead of time and refrigerate until use. If you will be putting them into warm soup or broth, place in hot water first, to warm them.

Apple Kugel

Yield: 6-8 servings

4 matzohs
3 eggs
1/2 teaspoon salt
1/2 cup sugar
1/4 cup melted shortening or butter
1 teaspoon cinnamon
1/2 cup walnuts
2 large apples, cored and chopped
1/2 cup raisins
A bit more shortening

Break matzohs into pieces and soak in water until soft. Drain, without squeezing. Beat together eggs, salt, sugar, melted shortening or butter, and cinnamon. Add to matzohs. Stir in chopped walnuts and apples. Add raisins. Place in an 8" or 9" square baking pan and dot with extra shortening. Bake at 350 degrees for 40-45 minutes, until light brown.

Mud Pies, Tea Parties— and More

by LaRene Wolfe

During World War II my family lived in a tiny old house on the east side of Denver. The sky was always filled with the sound of airplanes taking off and landing at Buckley and Lowry fields. The noise was muffled by many tall cottonwood trees, and by some gigantic old pines that shaded our house and yard.

The tall trees formed a leafy green umbrella over our house. It was an oasis where I played with my sister Jan. A climbing rose on the west side of the front porch also gave us shade. The adults had their own oasis where they sat when the day's work was done—our front porch. No one had air conditioning, or even an electric fan. We relied on nature for a cool breeze.

Because we had the only shady yard around, the neighborhood kids often came to play in the cool shade. Sometimes their mothers came to visit my mom. She always served them a cool cup of tea on our shady porch.

One year, I was about to go into second grade. My sister Jan was almost three. Most days, we played with the Towbin girls, Elaine and Jane. Elaine was about to go into first grade, and Jane was going into kindergarten.

Since I was the oldest, and it was my yard, I was the boss, and I got to decide what we would play. I loved to imitate how my mother baked goodies that made the house smell good. We made mudpies nearly every day. I pretended to measure the dirt and water ingredients. Elaine served water in little cups from her tin tea set. For guests, we used dolls. Jane dressed them up and spoke for them. Jan mixed the mudpies. For decorations, we filled jar lids with mud and made designs from juniper berries, clover blossoms, and pine needles.

A five-year-old named Ernie was the only boy on the block. He lived next to the Towbins. If he wanted to play with other kids, he had to join us girls. Instead of a doll, he had a well-worn teddy bear. We used Ernie as "Dad" for our games, so we didn't have to pretend that all the dads were away at the war. Besides, we had some "Dad" clothes in our dress-up suitcase.

Sometimes, when we wanted to get Ernie out of our way, we sent him off to "work" in the vacant lot next to my house. He was quite a sight pedaling his trike in my grandpa's big old shoes and wearing a fedora hat that come down over his eyes and rested on his ears. While Ernie was "at work" he collected supplies for making even better mudpies! He found an old rolling pin with one handle, some bottle caps that made great cookie cutters, and an old board on which we could display our mud creations.

Each of our yards had a different kind of dirt, which we could use for different things. My yard had soft dirt that we sifted through an old tea strainer to make "flour." The Towbins' yard had sticky clay soil that had been dug up when their home's foundation was made. We shaped it into "dough" that we rolled out to make cookies, or into squares for making "brownies" (with small rocks for "nuts"). Sometimes we rolled it into a snake shape and cut slices with an old butter knife, just like my mom did when she made "Icebox Cookies" from my grandma's recipe.

Back then, most people didn't have refrigerators. They kept things cold in an "icebox," a heavy wooden cupboard with a tin-lined top shelf. A man called the "iceman" came to our house each week with a big truck loaded with chunks of ice. He would carry in a big hunk of ice and put it in the top shelf to keep the food on the other shelves cold. We kids used an old fruit crate as a pretend icebox, and an empty shoebox for a block of ice.

There were lots of new homes being built in our neighborhood. Ernie filled a tin can with sand that was being used to build new sidewalks. We used it for our pretend sugar. (It was especially valuable because real sugar was rationed because of the war, and our mothers used it sparingly.)

Because Ernie helped by finding "sugar," one day we girls decided to let him stay home from "work" and make mudpies with us. We ignored the fact that he was a boy until dress-up time. (More on that later!)

Every day we had more and more fun, as we came up with new ways to make and decorate mudpies. When the cottonwood trees showered down their seeds, we used them for whipped cream filling and frosting. We used dandelion blossoms, and other weeds from vacant lots, to add variety to our creations.

As we grew older, we continued to make mudpies, and to have tea parties. One memorable one was a couple of years later, when we had a "special tea party" to celebrate something wonderful. My family was going to move into a new house on the west side of town—a house that we would OWN, rather than rent. Mom's friends told her they were glad we would have such a nice house, even though it meant we'd be moving away. She was happy to have such understanding friends.

The mothers finished their housework and put on their freshly ironed housedresses to gather for teatime. By now, families in some of the newer homes had modern electric refrigerators. Ernie's mom brought cool tea and ice cubes, and some extra cubes for us kids to suck on. Mrs. Towbin brought cookies that she made from my grandma's recipe (which my mom had shared with her). Jan and I still make these handy slice-and-bake cookies. But now we call them "Anytime Cookies," so we won't have to explain the original name of "Icebox Cookies."

To get ready for the party, we got out our dress-up suitcase. Elaine and Jane's auntie had given them some hats, gloves, and high-heeled shoes, along with some costume jewelry and a big purse. My parents contributed an old frayed white shirt and necktie for Ernie, and some old housedresses for us. We looked elegant in our tea party clothes. Ernie's mom even took our picture. Then, we gathered our dolls and Ernie's bear around a table (actually, a tree stump). Elaine set the stump table with her little tea set, and Jane and Jan dressed the dolls.

We took Mrs. Towbin's tea, and my mom's cookies, and used them for our tea party. We poured the tea into Elaine's tiny teapot. Then we put some of the smaller cookies on the plates of her tiny tea set. And we "baked" a big batch of mudpies, too!

We had a wonderful party. We had seen our mothers' good manners, and how they modeled the value of friendship over a good recipe and a cup of tea. We did the same. To make sure the dolls (and Ernie's bear) had good manners, Jane and Jan spoke for them, saying "Please pass the goodies," and "Thank you"—just like the adults, and just like us.

Soon, we moved into our new home. Our parents quickly met the grown-up neighbors, and we met the kids. Across the alley was a girl named Barbara. And three houses down the street was a boy named Roger. They were five years old, like Jan.

I liked our new house. The previous owners had planted an apple tree, so it had a lot of shade, where we played with our new friends. They quickly learned Jan's mudpie skills and our good tea party manners.

Seeing us enjoy a pretend party must have given the adults an idea. One warm evening, a neighbor invited everyone to her backyard to sample a new recipe that one of the ladies had seen in a magazine. This neighbor had a refrigerator. It was wonderful, because it let her keep ice cream frozen!

The dessert was a kind of pie made with a chocolate cookie crumb crust, and filled with peppermint ice cream. I loved it. It had a funny name, Grasshopper Pie. Roger's mom served the adults with her new hostess set, which was all the rage. It consisted of individual glass plates with a raised rim in which you put the cup to keep it from sliding. A guest could hold one of the plates in one hand and free up the other hand for eating, making sure to hold the plate level to prevent spills. Having the plates was great when she had so many guests that they couldn't all be seated at a table. She simply brought cups of coffee around to all the guests, whether they were sitting or standing. She also brought us kids small servings of a minty cool, creamy treat on toy plates. We imitated the adults, trying to keep our plates and cups level and not spill even one delicious bite.

We enjoyed that tea party so much that the next day, we had one of our own, featuring our own new mudpie creation. The grownups may have had Grasshopper Pie. But we had something even better—Live Grasshopper Pie! Jan lined a toy pie pan with mud and rolled out a mud top crust for it. Meanwhile, the rest of us kids went with tin cans to catch grasshoppers. When we caught them, we put our hands over the tops of the cans. You could hear "ping, ping, ping" as the insects tried to escape.

We came back to our table. Jan said, "One, two three!" and we all dumped the contents of our cans into the toy pie pan. As the grasshoppers fell, Jan tried to slap them into the pie crust. The grasshoppers escaped, while we leaped wildly after them. Of course, we wouldn't really have eaten the grasshoppers. But we had great fun making our pretend one-time creation.

By this time, I was old enough to learn to bake. The war had ended, and many ingredients that had been rationed no longer were. By then, school had started. Since we had moved, I was going to a new school. I was glad that I made a new circle of friends. We were all about nine years old. We formed a club that met after school once a week at each other's homes. We played board games and card games, and, most importantly, we had refreshments!

Each household had its own special kind of homemade goodies. Ours was Grandma's Icebox Cookies, which we served and ate warm. The girls in our club all liked to play dress-up. We all had some cast-off clothing and accessories that we got from our parents. We had great fun borrowing or trading clothes, and decking ourselves out weekly for TEATIME! We prided ourselves on our elegant manners as we passed the treats around and imitated the grown-ups. We never had to be reminded to say

"Please pass the goodies," or "Thank you."

The years passed. As we grew older, we learned more hostessing skills. By the time we reached our teens, we invited other guests to our tea parties—BOYS! Our school had Friday night dances in the gym. We had "Coketail Parties" in the girls' homes before the dances. Now, we imitated the adults' cocktail parties, instead of tea parties. Of course, we felt very sophisticated!

At our parties, we served Coca Cola. We made fancy sandwiches by cutting the crusts off slices of Wonder Bread and cutting the sandwiches into four triangles. Since food and girls were involved (two of their favorite things), even the gangly teenage boys that we invited were willing to act like adults and balance a fancy glass plate with a glass cup of cola and an assortment of goodies on it. And the boys had good manners. Even though their voices were changing and they sometimes squeaked, they never forgot to say

"Please pass the goodies," and "Thank you."

Some years later, when I was teaching second grade, my class read a story about a tea party. The girls knew about tea parties, but not one of the boys was so privileged. The next day, during math, we had a Class Tea Party. The students all learned to measure so we could have lemonade and Rice Krispies squares. They did a great job. I was amazed at how accurately they poured four ounces of lemonade per child and measured and cut their Rice Krispies squares.

Now that I'm a grandma, I have lots of fun preparing tea parties with my grandchildren. On one of my kitchen walls, I have a big collection of cookie cutters. My granddaughters agree with me that everything tastes better when it's tiny and is served on miniature dishes. My grandsons love to make roll-and-cut cookies in the shape of fish. They hang a sheet over two chairs to make a "tent." Then they "camp out" in it, using their toy camping dishes. Sometimes, we put miniature marshmallows on toothpicks and pretend to toast them. It's not exactly a tea party, but I love helping them with it anyway.

Even though Jan and I aren't kids any more, we still make those wonderful "Icebox Cookies" that we had at our pretend tea parties. We love how you can slice and bake them, and fill the house with a wonderful aroma—all on a minute's notice.

And believe it or not, many other grownups that we know love how having a miniature tea party can make any occasion in their life special. My mom is now "Great Grandma." She and her friends really perk up when Jan and I show up (kind of like Red Riding Hood), dressed in purple dresses and red hats, and carrying a basket of goodies and some pretty little cups.

This story is a tribute to my friends, past, present and future, and especially to the many generations of my family who have shared stories and tea parties.

You know what? Right now is a good time for a tea party! Come on, everyone is invited!

"PLEASE PASS THE GOODIES."
"THANK YOU."

Anytime Cookies
(formerly Icebox Cookies)

1 stick butter
1/2 cup brown sugar
1/2 cup white sugar
1 egg

2 teaspoons vanilla
1-1/2 cups flour
1/2 teaspoon baking soda
1/2 teaspoon salt

1. Cream together butter, brown sugar, and white sugar.
2. Add egg and vanilla, and mix well.
3. Sift together flour, baking soda, and salt.
4. Combine dry and wet ingredients to make a firm dough. Divide dough into two parts.
5. Make two rolls of dough about 1-1/2 inches in diameter and roll them in waxed paper or plastic wrap.
6. Chill for at least one hour.
7. Heat oven (or toaster oven, for a very small serving) to 350 degrees F.
8. Slice dough in 1/4 inch slices and place on an ungreased cookie sheet about 2 inches apart.
9. Bake until edges start to brown.

Note: If desired, you may store dough in refrigerator for a week, or in freezer for a month, before baking.

Roll-and-Cut Cookies

5 cups flour
2 cups sugar
1 cup butter (2 sticks)
1 cup milk
4 teaspoons baking powder
4 eggs

Dash of salt
Choice of flavoring:
    1-1/2 teaspoons vanilla, OR
    1/4 teaspoon lemon extract, OR
    1/2 teaspoon orange rind

Mix all ingredients well. Cover and put in refrigerator overnight. Roll 1/4 of dough out on a lightly floured surface to about 1/4 inch thick. Cut into shapes with cookie cutters to fit the theme or holiday. Repeat with rest of dough. Bake on a lightly greased cookie sheet at 375 degrees F for about 10 minutes. Makes about 36 4-inch cookies or about 72 2-inch mini-cookies.

The Reluctant Student

by Lois Burrell

When I was five years old, my mother took me to visit Mrs. Neolus Pierce. Miss Nee, as she was called, was a large woman who weighed about 350 pounds. She walked with the aid of a cane. Miss Nee gave private music lessons in her home to people in the town. She also played the huge pipe organ at the First Baptist Church.

I can still remember seeing Miss Nee at church services. The pipe organ was on the front wall of the church. It had three rows of keyboards and huge gold-colored pipes that loomed above it, behind the pulpit. When Miss Nee played high notes, the sound came from the shorter pipes. When she played low notes, they boomed out of the big pipes. Sometimes, Miss Nee shook the church with the low notes.

And she could shake the church with her voice, too. Every Sunday morning, you could hear her strong bass voice drowning out the choir, as she sang "HOLY HOLY HOLY LORD GOD ALMIGHTY!!" She loved God, and she loved church music. They were the foundations of her life.

That first day at Miss Nee's house, she and Mother chatted for a few minutes, exchanging pleasantries. Then, Miss Nee told me to sit at the piano. She placed my right hand on the keyboard, with my thumb at middle C. She then showed me how to play C-D-E-D-C. For fifteen minutes, I played C-D-E-D-C. For thirty minutes, I played C-D-E-D-C. For forty five minutes, I played C-D-E-D-C. For one hour, I played C-D-E-D-C.

In my five-year-old wisdom, I finally announced that I had never seen anyone play C-D-E-D-C on the piano, but I had seen plenty of people playing the piano with two hands. I then gave a demonstration of how it should be done. Miss Nee told me that those people were playing "big music." She told me I needed to start with "little music," C-D-E-D-C, and then work my way up to big music.

As my mother and I walked silently home, thoughts were racing through my head. I was NOT going to be sitting at a piano for sixty boring minutes practicing C-D-E-D-C. I was going to be outdoors playing with my friends.

A few days later, my mother told me that Miss Nee wanted me to come back. She wanted me to hear a little boy, who was one of her students, play the piano.

I obediently trotted over to Miss Nee's house with my mother. She and Miss Nee chatted for several minutes while we sat and waited for the little boy. Fifteen minutes passed. The little boy did not show up. Miss Nee kept saying, "He should be here any moment now." Thirty minutes passed. Still no little boy.

Finally, Miss Nee said, "I guess the little boy isn't going to come today. Why don't you sit at the piano and play the notes that I taught you last time?"

I looked at my mother. I could tell that I didn't have any choice. I slid onto the piano stool and played C-D-E-D-C, C-D-E-D-C, C-D-E-D-C until Miss Nee told me to stop. I guess it took about fifteen minutes. But it seemed like forever!

"Good," said Miss Nee. "Now, to make it a little more interesting, let's add something."

She reached over and showed me how to play C-D-E-E-D-C. I didn't think it was any more interesting than C-D-E-D-C, but I didn't dare tell her that. So for the rest of the lesson, I played C-D-E-E-D-C.

When we finished, Mrs. Nee put a surprised look on her face.

"Well," she said. "The little boy didn't come today for some reason. But surely he will be here next week." She smiled at me. "Why don't you come back and hear him then?"

As soon as we were outside, I looked up at my mother. "Miss Nee doesn't have any little boy for me to listen to," I said. "She's just trying to trick me into taking piano lessons. I'm not going back!"

To my surprise, my mother didn't argue with me. That was the end of my piano lessons until I reached the age of nine. One day, a friend of mine named Estelle Combs rushed over to my house. She drew herself up straight and announced in a very superior manner, "I'm going to start taking piano lessons from Mrs. Neolus on Monday."

So, on the Friday before that Monday, I was back at the piano in Miss Nee's studio, playing C-D-E-E-D-C. But now I had a reason for putting up with the lessons—I wasn't going to let Estelle be a better piano player than me!

For the next eighteen months, we both took lessons from Mrs. Nee. We were friends, and we saw each other every day, so we always knew what the other one was playing. We discussed how we were doing, and we played the music from our lessons for each other.

But through it all, we were very competitive. We were both determined to stay ahead of each other in our lesson book. As time went on, the music got more interesting. I was happy that I was finally playing "big music." Even when I got bored, I kept on practicing.

After a year and a half, Estelle announced that she had stopped taking lessons. I think she expected that I would stop, too. But by then, to my own surprise, I was actually enjoying going to Miss Nee's house. I have to admit that the reason wasn't entirely musical. By that time a boy, who was about a year younger than I was, had started taking lessons right after mine.

Joseph Jones was cute, mischievous, and extremely talented. He could listen to any song on the radio and immediately sit at the piano and play it note for note. This was called "playing by ear." If Miss Nee was not in the studio when he arrived, Joseph would ask me where she was. Between students, Miss Nee usually went into the kitchen to eat a snack. One of her favorites was sweet potato pie. If she was in the kitchen, Joseph would light up the piano with a boogie woogie, jazz, or rhythm and blues tune. The sounds would float from the studio and into Miss Nee's ears in the kitchen. She would make double time coming out of the kitchen on her cane, while yelling "Get that mess out of my house!" Miss Nee only approved of classical music and church songs. She also detested "playing by ear." In her opinion, real musicians read and played music from notes.

I continued to take piano lessons from Miss Nee until I graduated from high school. She said I was her favorite student. My mother, who had taken piano lessons for ten years, was proud as she could be.

Joseph Jones went on to become a professional musician. He was an arranger and pianist for a famous group called "The Platters." They were one of the top vocal groups of the 1950s, selling more than 53 million records. An early version of the group, called "The Penguins," became one of the first black acts to crack the top ten on the pop charts, with the song "Earth Angel (Will You Be Mine)." The group's first recording as the Platters was "Only You (And You Alone)." That song went to number one on the rhythm and blues chart and crossed over to the pop chart, where it reached number five. Their next song, "The Great Pretender," brought them even greater success. When it topped the charts in 1956, the Platters became the first black act of the rock era to reach number one on the pop chart. Other big hits by the Platters were "Twilight Time," "Smoke Gets In Your Eyes," and "Harbor Lights."

I always made a point of visiting Miss Nee whenever I went home. During one visit, I excitedly asked her about Joseph.

"Isn't it great about Joseph Jones?" I said. "He arranges and plays piano for The Platters!"

Miss Nee looked up from the sweet potato pie she was eating. She gave me a look of disgust and disbelief. "Worst mess I ever taught!" she sniffed.

Once, when I returned home for a class reunion, one of my classmates told me that Joseph Jones would be playing the piano in town that weekend. He suggested that we go to see him. It was great to be with Joseph again and recall the good old days. That was the last time that I ever saw him, as he unfortunately experienced an untimely death.

My mind often wanders to thoughts of Joseph. I love to remember his mischievous manner. I also think of him whenever I see sweet potato pie. Mostly though, I grieve for the loss of his special talents to myself and the entire world.

Miss Nee's Sweet Potato Pie

Crust:

2 cups flour
1/2 teaspoon salt
1 egg, beaten
3 tablespoons cold water
3 oz. butter

Filling:

2 cups sweet potatoes, canned
1-1/4 cups sugar
3 eggs, beaten
1 teaspoon cinnamon
1 teaspoon nutmeg
1/2 teaspoon salt
1/2 stick butter (do not substitute margarine)
1-1/2 cups milk

Crust: Sift flour and salt together. Mix with other ingredients until the consistency of cornmeal. Add water to bind. Roll out on a lightly floured board. Place in a 9-inch pie pan, and flute edges.

Filling: Drain liquid from can of sweet potatoes. Mash potatoes. Combine potatoes, sugar, and eggs. Beat with a mixer until smooth. Add cinnamon, nutmeg, salt, butter, and milk. Mix thoroughly. Pour into pie shell. Bake at 350 degrees on bottom rack of pre-heated oven for 60 minutes.

Root Beer

by Susan Marie Frontczak

The summer my cousin Andy turned seven, and I six, he and I started searching our alleyways for discarded treasures. Our primary goal was to find pop bottles. Andy built a massive comic book collection by turning in his bottles for two cents apiece. I scavenged pop bottles too. But I didn't cash them in, tempting as it would have been to pocket the change. I saved the bottles I found, so my family could use them to brew root beer.

One Saturday, a couple of weeks after school let out for the summer, Daddy said, "It's time." My older sister Emily (who was nine) and I followed Mommy and Daddy down to the basement to gather our root-beer-making supplies.

"Here, Emily," Mommy said. "You carry the bottle capper."

She turned to me. "Susan, here are the bottle caps, and don't let them spill." I clasped the box of miniature gold crowns to my chest. I felt rich, because they rattled like loose change.

Daddy pulled out an aluminum vat that looked big enough to crawl into. He looked at us and said, "You could take an n-a-p in this p-a-n." We all laughed, because we knew Daddy loved playing with words. Mommy went to the kitchen and brought out up a huge spoon, a funnel, a ladle, and a big pitcher for measuring water.

We carried the equipment out to our wooden picnic table in the back yard. Mommy went back to the kitchen for a bag of sugar, the tiny brown magic bottle of root beer extract, a box of raisins, and a mysterious little block wrapped in foil. Daddy carried out the boxes filled with pop bottles, which Mommy had sterilized in boiling water.

After we set everything out, Mommy poured the whole five-pound bag of sugar into the big vat. Astonished, I watched the mountain of crystal white sugar pile up at the bottom—more sugar than I could ever imagine in one place at one time. Next, Emily proudly poured in the root beer extract, a thick, sticky brown liquid that smelled like wintergreen and licorice. We took turns stirring until our arms grew weary and the sugar turned a sparkly brown.

Next, Mommy measured in the water with the pitcher. Now we really had to stir, to dissolve all the sugar. Daddy helped me when it was my turn. I liked feeling his strong arms and hands as I stirred, stirred, stirred. He tickled my ear and whispered, "Don't stir from here, my sweet, until the sweets are stirred!" We stirred until the liquid was a clear brown, with no sugar at the bottom.

By the time the sugar had been stirred in, I was thirsty. I asked Mommy if I could have a sip.

"Okay," she said, "but you might not like it."

I couldn't understand why. It looked like root beer, and it smelled like root beer. But when I tried the little glass she poured for me, I wrinkled my nose. "Yechh!" I said, "It tastes like sugar water, not pop!"

Mommy smiled. "That's because we need to add one more ingredient. It's called yeast. It's a kind of good germ that will help us make the root beer. The yeast comes in this little block wrapped in tin foil. Believe it or not, it's alive."

She brought Emily and me into the kitchen. "First, we'll warm up a little water, to dissolve and proof the cake of yeast. If it's still alive, as it should be, it will make tiny bubbles. Be we have to be careful—if the water's too hot, it will kill the yeast." She dissolved the cake of yeast in the warm water.

I watched and waited. The bowl just looked like a beige slimy mess. I watched and waited some more. And then, "Look!" I said with excitement. "There are some bubbles!"

"Okay," said Mommy. "The yeast is still alive. Let's put it in."

"Why does the yeast have to be alive?" I asked.

"That's what makes the root beer-flavored sugar water taste like pop," said Daddy. "The yeast will eat some of the sugar and give off bubbles made of a gas called carbon dioxide. The carbon dioxide bubbles make the root beer fizzy." Emily and I helped Mommy and Daddy mix the bubbly yeast into the sugar water.

"Now it's time to bottle," said Mommy. "Can you drop two raisins in each bottle, Susan?"

I picked up a fistful of raisins and started plopping them in. "Why do we put raisins in the bottles?" I asked. "When we buy pop at the store, it doesn't have raisins in it."

"Remember how the yeast makes bubbles?" asked Mommy. I nodded.

"The bubbles help us know when the root beer is ready. When there aren't many bubbles, the raisins sit at the bottom of the bottle, and the root beer would still taste like sugar water. We'll check every day. When there are enough bubbles to lift the raisins to the top, the root beer is fizzy and ready to drink."

"Can I be the one who watches to see if the raisins are at the top?" I asked. "I'll check every day. I promise!"

"Okay. But remember, it's a very important job. If we wait too long, the yeast will eat all the sugar, and the root beer won't taste sweet any more."

"That's right," advised Emily, who was older and had done this before. "But there's another reason you have to be careful!"

"What's that?" I asked.

"Get this," she said. "The bottles can explode from having too many bubbles if you wait too long!"

My eyes grew wide with shock. I looked at Daddy to see if what Emily said was true.

"Yes," said Daddy, "If you wait too long, the fizz will go WHIZZ!" We all laughed.

Mommy moved us along. "Emily, can you help me fill the bottles? We need to be careful not to overfill them! We want to leave about an inch at the top."

Mommy and Emily filled the bottles, one at a time. Mommy held the funnel so it was sticking down into the bottle. With the ladle, Emily ever so carefully poured just enough root beer mixture down through the funnel.

"Let me try!" I said. But when I tried it, the bottle overflowed. What a sticky mess!

"Susan," said Daddy, "Could you cap the bottles? Put one cap on top of each bottle, and stamp down the bottle capper."

Daddy hoisted me onto the picnic seat bench where I could get leverage enough to pump down the handle of the bottle capper. He wrapped his big hand over mine, and together we crimped the gold crown cap on the top of each bottle. It felt like magic to me. We had made a real bottle of pop!

Soon a small army of brown bottles filled the table. "All that's left," said Daddy, looking at me, "is to watch for the risin' raisin."

Finally, we rinsed off the sticky table, vat, funnel, and ladle with the hose. When we finished, we sat down for Leftovers Night, just like every Saturday. Mom pulled all the containers that had just one or two servings out of the refrigerator. There were over a dozen. She heated them up on the stove.

If Emily or I ate the last of a leftover dish, Mommy or Daddy said, "You get a gold star!" They didn't really give us gold stars. But their praise felt as good as the real ones that we got in school. We competed to see who could earn the most. Sometimes one of the leftovers made me hold my nose. But if there was only a little left in a dish, I might go ahead and eat it to get the reward!

When we finished, Daddy eased back in his chair. He patted his full tummy and said, "Bread rises in the yeast, but goes down behind the vest." We laughed, because we knew that the sun rises in the East and goes down in the West. Daddy was making fun of his tummy.

The next morning, we placed the bottles in the sun on the warm grass. "The yeast hibernates if it's cold," Daddy explained. "But it wakes up and makes bubbles when it's warm." Emily and I prayed for hot days, sunny days, to ripen the root beer.

Just like I promised, I checked the raisins every day. Mommy taught me to gently rotate the bottles, to keep the yeast mixed. Day after day, I peered at the bottles, only to see the raisins still sulking dully at the bottom. I sulked too. I was sure the raisins would never rise to the top!

Finally, after days and days (which seemed like years), one raisin floated to the top of its bottle. I picked up the treasure and rushed into the house. "It's ready!" I shouted. "It's ready!"

Our family opened and shared the first bottle that evening. It whetted my taste for more.

Once that bottle got fizzy, more ripened every day. Eventually we had to cram as many bottles as we could into the refrigerator, in an attempt to slow down the yeast. We had so much root beer that on the 4th of July Mommy and Daddy said that Emily and I could drink as much as we liked! I asked right away for a root beer float with vanilla ice cream.

As we indulged in our abundance of root beer, Mommy raised a glass as a toast to Daddy. She winked.

"Why is the 4th of July?" she said.

Daddy thought for a second, then smiled. "Yes," he said, "you're right!"

I said he was very silly to answer a question by saying "You're right."

Then Mommy said it again: "Why is the 4th of July?" Emily tried to tell her about the Declaration of Independence. Mommy shook her head and put on a very serious look. Then, she wrote "JULY" on a piece of paper.

"Look," she said. "Y is the 4th letter of the word JULY!" I grimaced. There must have been something in the root beer—now Mommy was making puns, too!

Over the years, my root-beer-making assignment changed. When I reached ten, the job of dropping the raisins into the bottles passed to my baby brother Michael, who was two. By the time I hit twelve, Dad let me cap the bottles with my own strength. When I was fourteen, Mom challenged me to calculate exactly what mix of 8-ounce and 12-ounce bottles we needed for four gallons of root beer (it was now my job to wash the bottles). By age sixteen, I bottled root beer with friends. Dad watched as I grew. Every year, at root beer time, he'd say, "The raisin's not the only one that's risin'."

§§§§§

Eventually I went off to college, and after that I became an adult and went to work every day. I forgot about making root beer in the back yard. Those memories might have been lost forever if I hadn't come back on a business trip and spent a few days at my folks' home. I hadn't been there in twelve years.

By now, Dad couldn't work any more. He had recently been diagnosed with a sickness that makes it hard to remember things, especially things that had happened recently. It's called Alzheimer's disease. With pieces of his memory gone, Dad did his best to make do with the things he could remember and understand. He had lost his job and his pension a few years earlier, before anyone understood that he was sick. So my mom, who used to teach piano lessons at home, started working full time as a business manager at a local medical clinic.

One morning, before going off to work, Mom went down to the basement. She brought up the dusty old bottle capper that I had been so proud to stamp down on the gold crowns so many years before. "I thought you might want to have this," she said. "We haven't used it in years."

After Mom drove away, Dad sat down at a jigsaw puzzle. Normally his attention was short these days, so I was amazed to see him sit at that puzzle for over two hours! I guess his lack of short-term memory let him forget how long he had been sitting at the table. He always had just enough attention to look for one more piece.

To give him a break I said, "Dad, let's go outside." It was late summer, and some of the leaves had started to fall. With his limited ability to grasp the bigger picture, Dad walked around the yard, picking up one leaf at a time. This struck me as a strange echo of the puzzle pieces he'd been handling a few minutes before.

Around lunchtime, we came inside. Dad opened the refrigerator to rummage for food. He took out a bottle of soy sauce. It had about an inch of brown fluid in the bottom. "Would you like some root beer?" he asked. "You'll get a gold star if you finish this in one gulp."

It was just the kind of joke Dad had always loved to make. I started to laugh, almost gagging at the thought of swigging soy sauce for a gold star. But then I stopped. He looked at me, his face empty, guileless. All of a sudden I realized that he didn't understand that he had just made a joke. His brain's jigsaw puzzle had lost pieces that would never be found again. I gave him a great big hug, knowing I would always treasure this, along with my other root beer memories.

frontezak family Root Beer Recipe

KIDS—If you use this recipe, have a grownup help you!

Equipment

Large vat
Large spoon or paddle
Funnel
Ladle
Enough glass bottles for 5 gallons of liquid, cleaned in boiling water

Bottle capper and new (unused) bottle caps.

(NOTE: Some folks today use cleaned and rinsed plastic bottles and caps; a bottle capper is then not required.)

Ingredients

4 pounds sugar (about 9 cups and 2 tablespoons)
One 4-oz. bottle of root beer extract
4-3/4 gallons of cold fresh water (or as instructed on the bottle of root beer extract)

1/2 cup warm water
One 0.6-oz cake of fresh yeast, OR 1 packet of dry yeast
Raisins (one or two per bottle)

CAUTION:

• In step 7, place bottles in a place that will avoid injury to people or animals if a bottle should explode. See the next bullet point in this caution for how to avoid having this happen.

• After raisins rise in the bottles (step 8), or after you feel pressure building up in plastic bottles (step 8), IMMEDIATELY refrigerate the bottles. DO NOT LEAVE BOTTLES IN A WARM PLACE—THEY MAY EXPLODE!

1. Pour the sugar into the vat.
2. Add root beer extract and stir to mix evenly.
3. Add about 4 gallons of the water. Use some of the water to rinse out the bottle of root beer extract several times, to get all the extract into the mix. Stir, stir, stir to dissolve all the sugar.
4. Warm up the 1/2 cup of water, but not too hot! Dissolve the yeast in it, using the spoon. Wait a few minutes, until little bubbles form on top of the yeast. Add the yeast mixture to the vat, and stir to mix.
5. Add the last 3/4 gallon (3 quarts) of water, using some to rinse the yeast cup into the vat. Stir.
6. Put one or two raisins in each bottle. With the funnel, fill each bottle with the root beer liquid, leaving an inch at the top. If you have different size bottles, fill the larger ones first. Cap the bottles.
7. Leave the bottles in a warm place (room temperature, or out in the sun).

8. Wait until the raisins float to the top (glass bottles) or until bottles start to feel hard with pressure, even if the raisins haven't risen (plastic bottles). This will take between four days and two weeks.
   NOTE: If you're using plastic bottles, IMMEDIATELY refrigerate when bottles start to feel hard with pressure!
9. Refrigerate until served.

CAUTION:

- When opening root beer bottles, OPEN SLOWLY TO SAFELY RELEASE PRESSURE
- Point bottles AWAY FROM PEOPLE AND PETS when opening.

Alternate Root Beer Recipe

I've modified my old family recipe, with thanks to David Fankhauser at http://biology.clc.uc.edu/fankhauser/Cheese/ROOTBEER_Jn0.htm in recognition that glass bottles and bottle cappers are not as readily available as they were many years ago.

KIDS—If you use this recipe, have a grownup help you!

Equipment

Clean, dry 2-liter plastic soft drink bottle, with cap
1-cup measuring cup

1/4-teaspoon measuring spoon
1-tablespoon measuring spoon
Funnel

Ingredients

1 cup cane sugar
1/4 teaspoon dry baker's yeast

1 tablespoon root beer extract
Cold, fresh water (best without chlorine)

CAUTION:

- In step 6, place bottle in a place that will avoid injury to people or animals if it should explode. See the next bullet point in this caution for how to avoid having this happen.

- In step 7, when you feel pressure building up in the bottle, IMMEDIATELY refrigerate it. DO NOT LEAVE THE BOTTLE IN A WARM PLACE—IT MAY EXPLODE!

1. With the funnel, pour the sugar into the 2-liter bottle.
2. Add the baker's yeast, and shake bottle to mix.
3. Swish the bottle around to make a dish shape in the sugar to catch the root beer extract. With the funnel, add root beer extract.
4. With the funnel, fill the bottle half way with clean water. Pour the water into the funnel over the tablespoon, to rinse the root beer extract that sticks to the spoon into the bottle. Twirl the bottle around until all ingredients are dissolved.
5. Fill the bottle with clean water, leaving an inch of air at the top. Cap the bottle and shake to completely dissolve all ingredients.
6. Leave the bottle in a warm place (room temperature).
7. Refrigerate the bottle as soon as it feels hard with pressure. This will usually take about four days.

CAUTION:

- When opening the bottle, OPEN SLOWLY TO SAFELY RELEASE PRESSURE.
- Point bottle AWAY FROM PEOPLE AND PETS when opening.

Olé! Posole!

by Renee Fajardo

For mi familia and mis amigos, as always! For S.G., who heard my stories long ago and said I should write more. For my seven chili peppers and the "Big Rista." You are all the spice of my life. For every season and for all times, may your chili bowls run over with love.

Posole

Posole is a magical dish served on special occasions in many regions of Mexico and the Southwest. Often served on Sundays and at Christmas, this rich fragrant soup was traditionally made from a pig's head and dried flint corn.

The process of making posole (or *pozolli*, as the Aztecs called it) goes back hundreds of years, to the indigenous tribes of Mexico and the Southwest. They soaked hard, flavorful field corn in a lime and water mixture until the kernels swelled, expelling the hard outer shell. They removed the tough outer germ by hand, then dried the kernels.

After Spanish explorers came, posole recipes became as varied as the peoples who inhabited the vast areas where posole is now celebrated. Chilis, spices, and various meats are now used, in unique combinations, to make regional signature posole dishes.

Today, posole is sometimes made with hominy (a softer, less flavorful corn); dried or fresh chili; and pork, chicken, or beef. Toppings include shredded cabbage, chopped onions, and oregano.

Olé! Posole!

This story is about *familia*, about traditions, hope, and love. It's about hard times, good times, and the comfort that *un buen tazón de posole* can offer.

My multi-cultural family has always been like a bowl of posole. Many cultures are reflected in the Lucero posole (named after *mi prima*, Joanna Lucero). Spanish, German, Mexican, Irish, Belgian, and Pueblo blood runs through our veins. We are Chicanos because the Indian and Mexican cultures have always predominated in our family celebrations and special foods. Posole is the cornerstone of our heritage.

On holidays, we went to visit my Auntie Lucy, who lived on Galápago Street in Denver. Mi *papi* John, mi *mamá* Barbara, mi *abuela* Esther, mi *bisabuela* Sarah, and my brothers were there. All of our *tios, tias*, and *primos* also came, to celebrate with music, dance, and food.

Everyone contributed something special to these grand *fiestas*. Tio Ralph sang ballads on the guitar, primo Napoleon and Papi played piano, Mamá made fried chicken, and my bisabuela Sarah made bread. Tia Lucy made the best *tamales* and finest *chili*, Tio Jake was the *tortilla* maker, and my beloved Abuela Esther made mouth-watering *enchiladas*. But it was my cousin Joanna who had the honor of making our most revered dish, posole.

We only had posole on very special occasions. One of these was at Christmas. Everyone looked forward to our *posole de navidad*.

One Christmas when I was seven and could finally see over the top of the kitchen table, I saw my cousin Joanna chopping onions and cabbage. I saw a huge pot simmering and gurgling on the stove. It filled the house with a heavenly scent. I knew she was cooking posole. She and the other women were also cooking enchiladas, tamales, beans, and chili. But everyone was waiting for a taste of the posole.

In the living room, Uncle Ralph was playing guitar, with his eyes closed in concentration. He played haunting melodies, some of them soft and gentle, others wild and loud. After each song, he paused. With a powerful voice, he uttered one word: "Olé!"

The third time I heard it, I ran to the living room. "Tio," I said, "what is that word? Why do you say it after every song?"

"Ah, *mija*," he answered. "It is a tribute. It is a word of honor and knowing."

"Tio Ralph!" I stammered. "How can a word know or honor anything? And you didn't answer me. Why do you say it when you finish a song?"

"'Olé!' means that times have been hard," he said. "The music I play is from our familia. It is about hard work, hard lives, hard choices, hard tortillas, hard bread, and hard breaks. 'Olé!' means 'yes.' We know about hard times."

He paused. "'Olé!' means your *bisabuelo* and his brothers once owned a great *rancho* and lost it. Then they worked in the dirt and darkness of the coal mines in southern Colorado, but they couldn't make enough money to keep the house warm. It means your tios and tias worked from sunup to sundown in the sugar beet fields of northern Colorado to help their parents put food on the table. It means our familia has fought and died in many wars to keep this country free. It means that until your papi, no one in our familia ever dreamed of going to college."

I didn't know what a college was, but I knew our familia was proud that my papi had gone to one.

"And it means," he said, "that we didn't have enough money to go to the doctor or to a dentist. It means that we wore rags for clothes and had holes in our shoes. It means your papi, your mamá, and all of us here and not here today have cried, sacrificed, and prayed for a better life for you, and for all the *niños* and *niñas* who will follow us."

It was true, I thought to myself. Times *were* hard. My cousin Bob, my favorite primo, was fighting in a war far away across the ocean. Uncle Ralph and Auntie Lucy both had children who had died. Grandpa Al had lost his brother in what everyone called the Great War, and Auntie Josie had died young. Earlier that morning at breakfast, I had seen three men who lived in the train yard and had no money, and who came every day to ask for food.

I ran to the kitchen and pulled on my cousin Joanna's apron.

"You must stop cooking the posole," I cried. "Times are bad. We should not be having a party. We should not be eating such good food when there is so much sadness!"

My cousin looked up from the onions. I couldn't tell if her tears were because of them, or because she was sad.

"Who told you that times are bad, mija?" she asked.

"Uncle Ralph," I said. "That's why he keeps saying that sad word after every song."

"What word is that?"

I stood on tiptoe to reach her ear. I whispered "Olé!"

Cousin Joanna stopped cutting onions. She wiped her hands. She looked me in the face and began to laugh. She laughed so hard she almost gasped for air.

Uncle Ralph stopped playing the guitar. He came into the kitchen and asked my cousin what was so funny. When she explained it to him, he started laughing too. Then Aunt Mary and Uncle George started laughing. Soon, the whole house was filled with hysterical laughter and people slapping each other's backs.

Finally, Uncle Ralph took me by the hand and patted my hair.

"*Mira*," he said. "Times are always hard. It is the way of the world. The *música* I play is old; I learned it from your bisabuelo Antonio, my grandfather. He learned it from his grandfather. It is from a place called Spain. The gypsies who played it there were hard-working people from many different places, as we are. They worked hard and struggled to make a good life for their families."

He smiled. "But life is not just work. When they were done working or needed comfort, they played music and ate together. After a great song, one that told about their hard work and struggle, they said 'Olé!' It meant they had triumphed. It meant they had survived."

Aunt Mary came over. "We cannot stop being a family because times are hard," she said. "We live and look to the future with hope. 'Olé!' means we are still here. It means we made it another day, and another sunrise will shine upon us."

Cousin Joanna chimed in. "We are a mixture of many different people, who all came here to have a better life. We remember and celebrate by carrying on traditions from all of our ancestors."

"Like what?" I asked.

She pointed to the simmering pot. "Posole is from our Indian heritage. Like the música, it shows our familia's unity and love. We go on because many people from many places fought hard to make sure that we had a chance at a good life. We honor our familia with song, music, food, and dance from the past, so that we can appreciate the future."

Just then, the doorbell rang. "Who could that be?" I thought. In my familia, everyone just walked in and sat down.

Aunt Mary turned as white as a ghost. "No," she gasped. "Not my son! Please, God, not my son!"

Uncle Avel went to answer the door. He was my *padrino* and my hero. I loved how he was always joking and laughing. But his hands shook as he turned the doorknob. When unexpected people rang the doorbell in our neighborhood, they always brought bad news. Usually, it was about the war. Someone had been hurt — or worse. I knew, because once I heard my parents talking about the time when a man in a fancy Army uniform visited the Martínez family down the street.

Fear ran through the house like electricity. I knew what everyone was thinking. It must be a man with a letter about Cousin Bob.

Uncle Avel cracked the door open. A slight whiff of fresh, crisp December air came into the living room. At the door was a man in a fancy gray-green Army uniform.

My uncle stood there, motionless. No one dared to breathe. Then the visitor pushed the door wide open. The room was filled with a rush of cold wind. The glimmering sunlight beat down on the man's back. His face was hidden in shadow.

Everyone pushed toward the door to get a better look at the stranger. He stepped in, over the welcome mat. His black leather dress shoes creaked sharply as they hit the cement step that led to the carpeted living room.

Suddenly, a deep, familiar voice boomed out. "What the heck! Doesn't anyone know how to say 'Merry Christmas'?"

It wasn't a stranger with a terrible message, after all. It was Cousin Bob, home from the war on Christmas Day! The house exploded with laughter, smiles, hugs, and kisses. It was an unbelievable Christmas gift.

A million excited questions filled the air. "How..." I heard, and "When..." and "Why didn't you tell us?" The smell of enchiladas, tamales, beans, chili, and posole wafted in, embracing the familia like a ribbon over wrapping paper. Along with the talking and laughing, I could hear music, and joyful singing. It seemed to go on forever, like a movie played in slow motion.

"Olé! Olé!" yelled Uncle Ralph as he beamed at Cousin Bob.

"Eat, eat," yelled Aunt Mary. "You look skinny, *mijo*. Don't they feed you there?"

The other women took up the chorus. "Are you hungry? What do you want to eat?" echoed through the living room.

My papi, my uncle Ralph, and my cousin Napoleon were our "family band." They started playing everyone's favorite songs. Folk tunes and cowboy songs, dance songs and smiling songs all blended into each other, like chocolate melting over ice cream on a hot summer day.

While they played the song "*De Colores,*" the women served bowls of posole to everyone. It was topped with chopped onions, shredded cabbage, oregano, and dried red chili flakes. Everyone was shouting and crying joyfully as they ate.

Cousin Bob got up. He hugged and kissed everyone in sight. He held up his bowl of posole and clanged his spoon on it to get everyone's attention. "*Feliz navidad!*" he shouted. Then he looked at Uncle Ralph.

"*Papá,*" he said. "you just played 'De Colores,' even though it's nowhere near spring. You know I wasn't here for my birthday last August. So I have a favor to ask. While we're eating our posole, I want to hear '*Las Mañanitas.*'"

I was surprised. Play a birthday song at Christmas? Grownups could be so silly!

Cousin Bob went on. "*Por favor,*" he said, "please, play it. For me. For us all. Play it loud and proud. *Con orgullo*. I missed it. I missed you all."

Uncle Ralph got up and grabbed his guitar. He played "Las Mañanitas," as the familia sang the words.

Some people started crying as they sang. I turned to Auntie Mary. "Why are they crying?" I asked. "I don't understand all the words in Spanish. But isn't it a happy song?"

She laughed. "Yes. But sometimes people cry because they're happy." Then she told me some of the words in English, as mi familia continued to sing.

> "How beautiful the morning is, and I come to share it with you. We are all here to celebrate this special day just for you. The day is dawning, and the light arrives in glory. Wake up, wake up on this beautiful morning to see all that we have done and accomplished. We are here to give you and your future joyful greetings!"

So that Christmas day, Uncle Ralph played "Las Mañanitas." It was Jesus' birthday, but he played it for Uncle Bob's missed birthday. It was a song for all of us, for all the birthdays in our familia. So we sang, as we ate our posole.

When the song was over, Cousin Bob got up. He raised his empty bowl up high and shouted "Olé! Posole!" Everyone looked at him in surprise. Then, all together, mi familia shouted back "Olé! Posole!" as they laughed and hugged.

I knew then that a new family *leyenda* had been born. Both the song and the soup would forever be etched in my memory. I knew that although times could be hard, there was "Olé!" It was a word of magic and hope and familia, a word to help us smile. My extended family spanned many generations and came from many different places. But "Olé!" meant the same thing for all of us. There is always a new day, a birthday, a new beginning, a new reason to rejoice.

Yes, times were hard. But in that little house on Galápago Street that Christmas Day, life was good, and peace was all around us.

Glossary:

Note: In the story, the *first* occurrence of each of the following Spanish words and phrases is in italics.

Abuela/Abuelo	Grandmother/Grandfather
Bisabuela/Bisabuelo	Great-grandmother/Great-grandfather
Chili	A kind of stew made with chili peppers or chili powder
Con orgullo	Proudly; with pride
De Colores	Spanish folksong; it begins "In colors, the fields are dressed in colors in spring"
Enchilada	A rolled, filled tortilla, covered with chili and usually baked
Familia	Family
Feliz navidad	Merry Christmas
Fiesta	Festival
Las Mañanitas	Traditional Mexican birthday song, which offers a good-morning wish
Leyenda	Legend
Mamá	Mother
Mi	My
Mija/Mijo	Short for *mi hija* (my daughter) or *mi hijo* (my son) but can be said to any young person
Mira	Look!
Música	Music
Niñas/Niños	Little girls/Little boys
Olé!	"Bravo!" or "well done!"
Padrino	Godparent
Papá; papi	Dad; Daddy
Por favor	Please
Posole	A traditional pre-Columbian soup or stew made from dried lime-treated corn kernels, often with meat, chili, and other seasonings and garnishes
Posole de navidad	Christmas posole
Prima/Primo	Female cousin/Male cousin
Rancho	Ranch
Tamale	Cornmeal dough rolled with ground meat or beans, usually seasoned with chili, wrapped in corn husks, and steamed
Tia/Tio	Aunt/Uncle
Tortilla	A thin, flat bread, usually made from corn meal or wheat flour
Un buen tazón de posole	A good bowl of posole

Cousin Joanna's Posole
(Serves 12)

Main ingredients:

2 cups blue dried whole hominy, or
    8 cups canned hominy
1 8-ounce can of diced green chilis
2 tablespoons crushed red chili pepper
2 tablespoons minced garlic
2 onions, chopped

1 14-ounce can of chopped, peeled
    tomatoes
2 to 3 pounds boneless pork roast, roast
    beef, or chicken breast*
2 quarts of water, or of chicken broth and
    water mixed half and half

*Posole can also be made without meat and is often served this way to accompany eggs at breakfast.

Garnish:

1/2 head cabbage, cored and finely
    shredded
1 bunch radishes, thinly sliced
1 onion, chopped
2 limes, quartered
Dried Mexican oregano, to taste

Cilantro, chopped, to taste
Parsley, chopped, to taste
Tostada chips or tortillas, cut into
    triangles and toasted, to taste
Bottled Mexican hot sauce or salsa,
    to taste

To make posole on the stove:
Dried hominy may be used for those who want a more traditional dish.

1. Rinse dried hominy or canned hominy under cold water until the water runs clear.
2. Soak hominy for several hours, or overnight, in cold water.
3. Place hominy in a large pot with enough water to cover it.
4. *Note: If using canned hominy, which is already cooked, skip this step. If using dried hominy, follow this step.*
   Bring water and hominy to a boil; reduce heat to low. Simmer, covered, until it pops, about one hour. Drain off any excess liquid.
5. If using meat, brown the meat in a separate pan.
6. Add all remaining ingredients to the pot, except salt.
7. Simmer, covered, for 4 hours (3 if using canned hominy).
8. If using meat, remove the meat, shred, and return to pot.
9. Add salt to taste.
10. Simmer, covered, 1 more hour.

To make posole in a crock pot:

1. Place everything except salt in a crock pot.
2. Cook for 6 hours on high, or 10 hours on low.
3. Add salt to taste.
4. If using meat, stir with a large spoon to shred the meat.

Olé! Posole!

My Story

My Recipe